THORRN

STARLIGHT HIGHLANDER MAIL ORDER BRIDES 1

SKYE MACKINNON

Peryton Press

CONTENTS

BEFORE WE BEGIN

This book has been written by a Scottish author and therefore uses British English (less Z, more S).

Trigger warning: Mentions of domestic abuse.

Subscribe to Skye's newsletter and get a free book as a thank you: **skyemackinnon.com/newsletter**

Thorrn is part of the Intergalactic Dating Agency multi-author project: **romancingthealien.com**

GLOSSARY

Many of the alien words are taken from Scottish Gaelic (yes, including the flying vagina). Some of them have been slightly changed, while others are exact translations.

Albya – planet of the Albyans (from Alba = Scotland)

Bainnse – wedding

Bawbag – scrotum (Scots insult)

Click – minute (30 Earth minutes are 20 intergalactic clicks)

C-suit – camouflage suit that helps aliens blend in with humans

Lady Beyra – Albyan Goddess (based on the Scottish/Celtic Beira myth)

Migges – midges (tiny mosquitos aka miniature demons who love to torment this particular author in her garden)

Pit air iteig – for fuck's sake (literally: flying vagina)

Rotation – Albyan year

Quantnet – intergalactic internet

Sgid/sgidding – fuck/fucking

Taigeis – a fluffy round animal based on the Scottish haggis

Ton air eigh dhut – fuck you (literally: may your arse hit the ice)

1

Jenny

My ex left me with a suitcase full of cut-up clothes, a key-scratched car and a broken arm. Good riddance.

I didn't realise he'd destroyed all my clothes until I sat in my brother's spare room. He'd taken one look at me, given me the biggest hug ever and told me I could stay for as long as I needed. My brother was the best.

That bastard Jason had done a great job. I only found a single top he hadn't torn to pieces. At least I'd never agreed to give up my own bank account. We'd had a shared one to pay for the rent, food and bills, but my savings were safe, ready to be drawn on until I was back on my feet.

"Dinner's ready!" Ewan shouted from downstairs. My stomach growled in response. My last meal had been yesterday evening, before the row that had ended in a trip to A&E. They hadn't let me eat in hospital just in case I needed an operation, but luckily the break was clean and needed only a cast. When I'd arrived back home in a taxi, I'd found a suitcase next to my Mini. SLUT was sprayed on both driver doors. Jason was nothing if not petty. I'd make sure to tell the police all about it when I went to give my statement tomorrow. If he wanted war, he could have it.

I slowly walked down the carpeted stairs, wincing at the pain in my thigh. I couldn't quite remember how I'd sustained the giant bruise. Maybe I'd bumped against the kitchen counter during the row. Not that it mattered. I gritted my teeth and ignored the pain.

The sight of a ginormous lasagne made me smile. Ewan always knew how to cheer me up. He was a cook by trade, making fancy food at one of the city's most exclusive restaurants, but when I visited, he always provided me with simple comfort food. As a bonus, I'd be able to eat the lasagne with just a fork, one-handed as I currently was.

"Smells delicious. Is Anna joining us?"

"No, she's working the night shift and won't be home until four. It's just us, little sis."

He grinned as he cut the lasagne in half. It would have been enough to feed a family of six, but I knew that the glass dish would be empty by the time we were done with it. He put a plate in front of me, so full that a trickle of cheese was slowly oozing onto the table. I picked it up and pulled a beautiful string of cheese, ready to be slurped like spaghetti.

Ewan chuckled. "I see you still haven't learned any table manners. Ma would be so disappointed."

"Ma would do exactly the same and you know it." Our mother was a hippie who'd married a simple crofter, giving us a unique upbringing far from the busy city we now lived in. Sometimes, I'd considered whether to move back to the Highlands, but there were no jobs there, at least not the kind of jobs I was interested in. One day, I might leave Glasgow for a smaller place, but for now, I was happy here. Well, except for my prick of an ex. I realised how quickly he'd changed from boyfriend to ex-boyfriend in my mind. I supposed it had been inevitable. All I'd needed was the right reason to leave. And a broken arm qualified for that.

"Do you want to talk about it?" Ewan asked after a few minutes of companionable silence.

"Not really. I'll have to tell the police tomorrow; I think that's enough."

"Well, you know I'm here whenever you want to talk. Day or night. And you can stay for as long as you need to. The room's been empty ever since Anna's mum moved to that assisted living place, so we have space. And I like cooking for you."

I laughed. "You'd think you'd never get to cook in your life."

"It's different making food for the people you love."

"I suppose so."

I'd never been as obsessed with food as my brother. I liked eating it, sure, but I was happy to let other people do the actual cooking. Jason hadn't been half-bad at it, but he'd always made sure to let me know what a failure I was at homemaking. It didn't matter that I earned more than him. In fact, it may have made things worse.

"How's the job?" Ewan asked. "Any interesting new projects?"

"Yes, actually. I've got a meeting tomorrow with the owner of a dating agency. Hot Tatties. They want a big marketing campaign to find more people to sign up. Apparently, my pitch really impressed them and they didn't blink an eye at the price of my premium package. I'll probably be working with them for a couple of months at least."

"A dating agency. Guess that'll help if you want to get over that bawbag quickly."

I shot him a look. "No, thanks. I've learned my lesson. I have the worst possible taste in men and I shall stay single for the rest of my days."

Ewan snorted. "Are you saying you're becoming a nun?"

"I never said I'd stay celibate."

He covered his ears. "I don't want to think about my little sister and sex. Ewww. Disgusting."

"You should know by now how sex works. Remember when I found those magazines under your bed?"

His cheeks reddened until they almost matched the colour of his hair, the same ginger hair I was cursed with, except that his was a lot shorter and less curly. "Stop it or I'll evict you."

Despite his jovial tone, I couldn't help but flinch. It was still all too raw and fresh.

"Sorry," he said immediately. "Not cool of me. I won't throw you out, ever. And you know how much Anna loves you. I'm pretty sure that if she hadn't married me, she would have taken you instead."

I laughed. "I discovered that I'm not into women, sorry."

"Discovered? How?"

"Didn't you experiment while at uni?"

He blushed even more. "Not really. Those were different times."

I rolled my eyes. "You're seven years older than me. Not enough to pretend that you're a different generation. So you never had a drunken thing with a guy?"

"Bloody no to the no. And if I did, I don't remember. In fact, I don't remember a lot of my uni days. I spent a lot of them hungover."

"And here I thought that you studied hard like ma always told me when she presented you as the ultimate role model. Maybe I should tell her..."

"Don't you dare. If you do, I'm afraid I might have to expose one of your secrets. But which one to choose? There are so many."

I flicked a piece of melted cheese at him while at the same time wondering what secrets he had about me. Not that I was a very mysterious person. I wore my heart on my sleeve most of the time, and I'd learned that playing poker was a quick way of losing money. I sucked at poker faces and keeping a hold on my emotions. At least that kept me honest. The only person I could successfully lie to had been Jason and that was mostly because he didn't pay much attention to me. When had I last had a proper conversation with him that didn't turn into a row? I couldn't say.

"You're thinking about him," Ewan said, proving my point. I couldn't hide anything from my brother. "He's not worth it. How about we open that bottle of Highland Park my boss gave me?"

"Your boss gives you whisky?"

"When I make her half a million quid with a deal, then yes, she does." He grinned proudly. "She let slip that I might get a promotion at the end of the year. We can use the money for decorating the nursery."

I gasped. "Nursery? Is Anna-"

"Not yet, but we're doing our best. Every day." He wiggled his eyebrows.

"I'm glad your bedroom isn't right next to mine. I don't need to hear my brother making babies."

"With Anna's current shift pattern, you don't have to worry about that. You'll be at work by the time she wakes up. I've been doing a lot of working from home recently." Ewan laughed. "I'm a lot more productive after a good shag."

He pulled a large bottle from the liqueur shelf. Our father was a big whisky fan and we'd grown up being dragged to distilleries across Scotland. After he'd seen them all, we'd started having family holidays over in Ireland. Right now, he was saving for a trip to Japan to visit some distillery he'd read about.

I swirled the golden liquid in my glass, resisting the temptation to go through the traditional steps of tasting whisky. My father had turned me into a connoisseur I didn't want to be. When I'd left for university, he hadn't warned me of staying away from horny boys and stuff like that. No, he'd warned me of the sin of mixing whisky with coke. I chuckled at the memory. Maybe I should take a few days off and visit my parents. A breakup was the perfect excuse. I didn't want to admit to them that I missed their company, hugs and even their advice. I was a grown woman, after all.

By the time Ewan refilled my glass for the fourth time, I'd almost forgotten about my broken arm, my bruises and the fact that I was currently homeless. I was happier than I'd been in months.

"You should go to bed," my brother said when I reached for the bottle again. His voice was slightly slurred. "You don't want to be hungover during your interview tomorrow." He looked at the clock above the kitchen door. "Today, actually. Time's moving so bloody fast when you're having fun."

"You're way too sensible," I complained.

"It's my responsibility as your big brother. Go on, bedtime. I need to grab a few hours of sleep too. I don't want to disappoint Anna tomorrow. That baby won't make itself."

I laughed harder than that joke was worth. Then cringed. Then wondered if I'd ever have a relationship as steady and loving as Ewan.

Probably not.

2

Jenny

The investigator shook my hand on the way out. "Thanks for your statement. I wish every victim of domestic violence would be as willing to come forward and give evidence as you."

"Not a victim," I said automatically. "And you don't have to thank me. I want him punished. Do you know how hard it is to put on a blouse while one of your arms is in a cast?"

She smiled. "Funnily enough, I do. How long do you need to wear yours?"

"Six weeks."

"Lucky. I had mine for ten. My arm looked like it didn't belong to me after they removed the cast, all pale and squashed. Prepare for lots of ingrown hairs."

She led me back to the reception area. "I'll be in touch as soon as I've talked to the CPS. This should be a relatively straightforward case, so I'm confident they'll decide to charge him. Your obvious injuries, as well as the statements from the neighbours, paint a clear picture that should lead to a conviction. We might have to do something called a victim personal statement at some point in the future, which is basically what we did today, plus giving you the chance to talk about how you've been affected by the abuse in the long term."

"Is he still in custody?" I asked.

"No, he's out on bail, but one of his bail conditions is that he's not allowed to make contact with you in any way. If he does attempt to get in touch, call me. If he turns up at your work or home, call 999."

"And he'll end up in prison?"

"I hope so. In the end, it depends on a lot of things. Best case, he'll get up to five years. Sadly, I've learned that we rarely get best-case scenarios. But as I said, I'll keep you informed. And please take advantage of the services mentioned on those leaflets."

She'd given me a whole stack of flyers about charities and services for victims of abuse. I was planning to throw them in the bin. Not a victim. I was fine. My arm would heal, my bruises would fade, and it would all be just a bad dream. I was rid of Jason and I wouldn't let him haunt me.

I left the police station with a smile. Maybe not the most natural reaction, but I was strangely happy and relieved. Now that this was dealt with, I could focus on more important things again. Like my job. I checked my smartwatch. I was running late to my first meeting with the dating agency. I'd planned to walk to their office, but it was time to splash out on a cab.

Pam's office was cosier than my living room had ever been. Fluffy cushions, a thick carpet, colourful wallpaper and beautiful curtains all worked together in creating a warm, welcoming space. A large kilt-wearing cupid hung on one of the walls, the agency's mascot.

She'd made a large pot of coffee, but I was more interested in the jaffa cakes she'd put in a bright pink bowl in the centre of the table. The office was big enough to accommodate both a desk at one end and a round table with two funky chairs on the other.

"Is this where you talk to your clients?" I asked while she was pouring me a cup.

"Yes, whenever possible. Some people prefer to chat on the phone, but I always like having a conversation in person. It helps a lot to get an accurate impression of them. Sometimes, people turn out to be very different from how they looked on paper."

"Makes sense. Will you be able to continue doing that, though? If this campaign is as successful as I'm planning it to be, you'll get a lot of clients very quickly."

Pam nodded. "I've hired two new girls to help me. And when I say girls, I mean that one of them is older than me." I estimated her to be in her late forties, with a few streaks of grey in her curly auburn hair. "I just signed a contract to rent out the flat above me and we're going to convert it to additional office space for them. In two weeks, all three of us will be able to welcome clients. Steff is moving from part-time to full-time, giving her the chance to deal with all the extra admin."

Steff was Pam's assistant. I'd not talked to her besides a friendly hello on the way in, but she seemed lovely. One of those cheerful people who made you smile as soon as you saw them. She was about my age, although she didn't have my frown lines and heavy bags beneath the eyes.

"I need you to make a change to the campaign," Pam said. "I only want to target females."

"Wait, no men? Why? Are you wanting to turn this into a lesbian agency?"

Pam grinned. "No, although of course we welcome all clients, no matter the preferences. I've been contacted by a different agency that only has guys on their books. They gave me a glimpse at their database and, oh my sweet little Cupid, our ladies are in for a treat. For some reason, they're only interested in Scottish females, so Hot Tatties is perfectly placed to work with them."

"That's amazing," I said while already mentally adjusting my plans for the advertising campaign. Targeting just one gender was going to be easier, but it might also mean a lower budget. "Why do they only want Scottish women? Are they some kind of nationalist group?"

For some reason, Pam cackled with amusement. "Not quite. They're...foreign, but with Scottish roots, and want to go back to their origins. Rekindle their culture or something like that. They were very clear in only wanting Scottish lasses, born and bred here. But they're in for a surprise. I won't discriminate against women with other backgrounds, so as long as they live in Scotland, they're welcome to sign up. Those guys will just have to learn to deal with it."

"The Scottish angle might be fun for the campaign," I mused. "Men in kilts will be great for social media. So drool-worthy."

"They're drool-worthy for sure. These guys wear kilts all day, every day, not just for special occasions like the men do here. And while I've not asked if they wear anything underneath..." She gave me a very suggestive wink. "I'm sure my ladies will be very pleased. I kind of wish I was single."

"Careful what you wish for," I muttered before I could stop myself.

"You're single?"

"Aye. Newly. And happily."

Pam gave me an understanding smile. "Well, if you want that to change, I can add you to the database. Free of charge. Actually, that might be a great way to give you a better idea of how we work. Yes, let's do it. If you know the process our ladies go through, you'll be able to convey the message better in your campaign."

"No, that's really not necessary," I said, but Pam was already grabbing her laptop, almost pushing her coffee cup off the table in the process.

"It's not serious if you don't want it to be," she reassured me. "You won't have to go on any dates, but I'll let you go through all the steps leading up to that. Agreed?"

She looked so enthusiastic that I couldn't say no. I'd always struggled with that, saying no. I knew some people took advantage of that, but in Pam's case, it wasn't malicious. She just enjoyed her job and wanted to share that joy with me. Oh well. As she said, I didn't have to meet any guys. But would it be so bad if I did? I shifted a little and the pain from my thigh gave me a very clear answer. No more men. Not for a while, anyway. Being single was a lot healthier.

"I've got a meeting with the head of the other agency tomorrow," Pam continued. "I'd like you to join us. I mentioned the campaign you're planning for us and they were very interested. Maybe it'll give you some more ideas now that the parameters have changed."

I didn't really need more ideas, my head was already swimming with them. Men in kilts. I could have them do all sorts of things. Exercise, yoga, weightlifting. Basketball or something where they had to jump, then do some shots from below, hinting at what might wait beneath the kilt...

I licked my lips. Tourists weren't the only ones who found kilts appealing. I wasn't talking about old guys at weddings. No, I was thinking of the kind of men you'd watch at the Highland Games, broad and burly and with thighs resembling the cabers they were throwing. Heat travelled down to parts that hadn't felt anything like that in way too long. Maybe going on a date with a hot Highlander wasn't a bad idea after all.

"How tall are you?" Pam asked, her eyes fixed on her laptop screen. "Five six?"

"Five foot five. Is height important to them?"

"Not that I'm aware. I just like to have all the details in case there are questions or special preferences. Usually, I'd take some pictures, but since this is just a test run, we can leave that unless you really want to."

"Nah, I'm fine." I much preferred being behind the camera.

"Alright, then you just have to fill in your hobbies, interests, what you're looking for in a man. You do that while I discuss something with Steff."

She handed me her laptop, leaving me to stare at the questions. I felt like this was an exam, worse than any I'd done at university. What were my interests? I'd had many before I'd met Jason. He'd become my one and only hobby.

The first few questions were what I had expected. What I did in my free time, my job, that sort of stuff. Typing was slow with just one hand, so I kept my answers as short as possible.

Would you be willing to relocate?

That was a hard one. Was I? A new start might do me good, away from everything that could remind me of Jason. I could do my work from home but-

Why was I even thinking about it? This wasn't real. I shouldn't put all this thought and energy into it. I randomly clicked the 'yes' box and continued on to the section about what I was looking for. I grinned. Let's have some fun.

Tall. Muscular. Kind. Sexy. Protective. Intelligent. Able to hold a conversation. Kilt wearer. Six pack. Large dick.

I deleted that last bit. It wasn't very professional and even though Pam was super nice, this was still a business relationship.

Thinking of my brother, I added 'good cook' instead.

Happy to share the house chores. Able to do DIY and use a power drill.

It was an inside joke. I'd once drilled a hole into my palm while using my dad's drill. I rubbed the scar. Ever since, I'd left DIY things to others. I wasn't to be trusted with sharp, dangerous, pointy devices that could bore holes into people.

"Are you done?" Pam asked. Lost in thought and memories, I hadn't even realised she'd returned.

"I think so. Not that it matters."

"No, but now you know what our clients have to do to be entered into our database. Once they've done that, it's time for the individual chat with me. Let's skip that, I'm sure you have other things to do. Do you need time to adjust your campaign so that it's only targeted to women, or shall we discuss it now?"

"Most strategies will stay the same, but I want to change our photoshoot to include men in kilts. The more Scottish, the better, right?"

"Definitely. And I want to come to that shoot. For purely professional reasons, of course." Pam grinned.

"Do you think it would be possible to get some of the males from the other agency involved? It would make it more realistic and show your prospective clients exactly what they might get."

"Let's ask in the meeting tomorrow. I've not actually met any of them in person yet; so far, it's all been online. They're flying in tonight and will stay for a few days until we've got everything agreed on paper."

"Where are they arriving from?" The only places with a history of Scottish emigration that I could think of were Nova Scotia in Canada and New Zealand. Probably the United States and Australia, too. A friend of mine had once sent me a postcard from New Zealand with a picture of their version of Ben Nevis. Funnily enough, our Scottish Ben Nevis was our highest mountain, but smaller than the Kiwi peak. That was the only reason I knew about a Scottish diaspora on the other side of the world.

Would moving to New Zealand be so bad? It looked amazing in pictures. It was really far away from my family, though.

You're not actually getting a sexy Highlander, I reminded myself. I had to stop pretending that I was really going to be in Pam's database.

"I'm not sure. They're coming by private plane, though. So posh. The way they mentioned that in passing made me think that they have a lot of money." She smiled happily. "Our cooperation will be a great boost for Hot Tatties. I might be able to give you a bonus at the end, if everything turns out well. Which I'm sure it will. What could go wrong with a campaign full of men in kilts?"

3

Thorrn

I glared at the blue planet quickly growing larger
beneath us. I didn't have time for this. I had a fight
to prepare for. I hadn't trained for months just to be
distracted by my brother's latest desperate scheme.
Unlike him, I'd long given up on our kind. Instead, I
lived in the moment. Fighting. Bathing in the adoration
of the masses. Challenging my body to the very limits.
And enjoying all the luxuries my prize money afforded.

Cyle, on the other hand, was the eternal optimist. He
still believed that we could find mates and ensure the
survival of our species. Somewhere in the galaxy, he
hoped, were compatible females. He'd dedicated his
life and career to the search for mates. We used to be
close, but our different perspectives on what was
important had made us drift apart.

Until now. I looked at him as he was snoozing on the seat opposite. As always, it was like staring into a mirror. We weren't twins but we were often mistaken for some. The same bright red hair that reached to our shoulders – although while he wore his loose, mine was braided tightly so it wouldn't get in the way during a fight; the same green eyes, the same freckles sprinkled across a broad nose. Of course, I was a lot more muscular than him, my body toned from years of training, but just like all Albyans, he had a naturally powerful build. His secondary arms were definitely thinner than mine, though. On the other hand, he still had both antennae. I'd lost my left one in a fight five years ago and my right one was permanently bent. Another reason why I wasn't keen on the whole mate thing. No female would consider a male without working antennae. How else would we sense our one true mate?

We were getting close to breaking through the atmosphere. I had to admit that the planet looked pretty from afar, a gorgeous ensemble of blues and greens covered by white stripes in places. Albya was mostly land with large lakes and rivers instead of oceans. Our planet was also a lot smaller than Peritus, or Earth, as the natives called it. Not that it mattered, with our population soon to be extinct.

"Arriving in fifteen clicks," the pilot announced. "It might get a little bumpy; the atmosphere's thicker than what we're used to."

I checked I was still strapped in properly, then closed my eyes. I hated landings.

With the chameleon shields engaged, we'd parked on a landing strip full of Peritan aircraft. They had a spaceport in this country, but it was primitive and nowhere near the city where we were going to meet the human female called Pam. Peritans had taken their first steps into space, but the Intergalactic Council hadn't opened up communications with their government yet. Technically, we were going against IGC law by visiting the planet, but Cyle and his colleagues were desperate. As long as we wore our C-suits, we'd look like the natives and it wouldn't count as First Contact. They were uncomfortable, especially because we had to keep our lower set of arms pressed against our bodies, but it was the only way to walk among the natives without sticking out as aliens.

If Cyle was right and we'd find compatible females here, we'd have to see what to do. It was the reason why he'd asked me to come along. For protection. Even though in the arena I fought with my four fists, I was well versed in both hand and spacecraft weapons. If worse came to worse, it was my responsibility to make sure my brother and the others were unharmed.

Not that I thought we'd end up with a fight. Peritans were puny and weak. I'd done some research during the flight here and wasn't impressed by their species. Still, even though Cyle and I had become somewhat estranged, I had no doubt he had a good reason for coming here. He was Albya's most eminent scientist and the Albyan Parliament had agreed to fund this research trip. I knew nothing about science and didn't really care. I was only here because Cyle had asked me. Begged me to come, even. As my only remaining family member, I hadn't managed to say no. Now we were on Peritus, a planet far from our own galaxy, looking for mates.

Cyle led us to a hotel not far from the airport. We got a few strange looks from Peritans, but our C-suits were working, I'd checked repeatedly. My brother had decided that our clothes were similar enough to what the natives wore, so all the C-suits hid were our antennae and secondary arms. We were taller than most Peritans, but according to Cyle, our height was still within natural parameters.

"Highland Games aren't until next month!" a male shouted. I wasn't sure what he was talking about, so I ignored him. He didn't seem like a threat. It was confirmation, though, that our BrainTrain language sessions had been successful. I understood him as well as if he was speaking Albyan Prime. All those nights wearing the itchy implants had been worth it.

A group of females on the other side of the street giggled and pointed at us. I strained my damaged antenna in their direction, just in case one of them was my mate. I wasn't sure if I'd even be able to recognise her with just one antenna. There were no females on Albya to practice on, at least not any awake. I felt no sexual attraction to the females trapped in the Sleep who were the only ones still alive.

"Do all their females look like them?" Jafar asked. He was Cyle's colleague who'd been instrumental in establishing contact with a Peritan owner of a so-called dating agency. I hadn't quite grasped the concept of it, but it seemed like they arranged relationships between mates. I had no idea how they did that. How could they match mates without them meeting each other? Peritans lacked mating antennae, but surely they had some other inbuilt mechanism to recognise their mates?

"I believe so, yes," Cyle said, staring at the females. "I hope so. Just look at those legs."

"Their legs? I'm admiring their breasts."

I chuckled. Of course, he would. Jafar was a scientist like Cyle, but he was less reserved and polite than my brother. Even if Cyle liked the female's breasts, he wouldn't say so because it wasn't proper. Our mother had made sure to teach us manners. We may have been without females for a long time, but neither of us had ever forgotten what she'd ingrained in us. Treat females with respect. Compliment them on their mind instead of on their body. Protect them without taking their independence. Still, I totally understood where Jafar was coming from. These females made my mouth water and my balls ache.

"Do you feel anything?" I whispered to Cyle, making sure Jafar couldn't hear me. Even though my disability was obvious, I didn't like to draw attention to my missing antenna.

"No, but they might be too far away. I'm not sure how close we have to get. We'll find out tomorrow when we meet with Pam. She's found mates for hundreds of Peritans. She'll know."

"A true expert then. How did you find her?"

"I hacked into their planetwide communications network called the world wide web. I don't know why they broadcast it into space, but I'd never have found Pam otherwise, so I won't complain. The Peritans must have their reason. Maybe they know about the IGC ruling and want to protest against being kept in the dark. Maybe it's their way to attract travellers and traders to their planet."

"I'll go over and tell them I like their breasts," Jafar announced. "Maybe that will activate my antennae."

I grabbed him by the arms. "No, you don't. We'll wait until our meeting tomorrow. We don't want to draw any attention to ourselves."

He grumbled under his breath but didn't make any attempts to join the females on the other side of the street. They were still shooting looks at us and it took all my willpower to ignore them.

Using the Peritan web technology, Cyle had booked us three rooms in a hotel. Vaxx, our pilot, had stayed back on the ship, making sure none of the natives stumbled across it by accident. He wasn't interested in females anyway, preferring the company of his own sex. Some days, I wished I was like him. I'd been with males, of course, most Albyans had to satisfy our urges, but it wasn't what I wanted and needed, deep inside. I may have resigned myself to being without a mate for the rest of my life, but that didn't mean my body didn't crave the physical aspects of mating.

The Peritan male at the hotel reception handed us a strange card each. "Are you here for a wedding?"

I exchanged a look with the others, hoping they'd know what he was talking about.

"No," Cyle said eventually. "We're here on business."

"Oh, right. I thought because of the kilts, you know. Don't get many people here wearing them at this time of year unless they're going to a wedding."

Pit air iteig! Cyle had been convinced that our traditional dress matched what the natives wore. It's why we'd come to this part of Peritus. The locals had strikingly similar looks and traditions which had made my brother hopeful that we'd find compatible mates here. Had our cover been blown not even twenty clicks after our arrival?

"We shall retire for the night," I said quickly and turned away from the Peritan, hoping the others would follow my lead. It may be slightly rude, but I didn't want to prolong this conversation.

"You're on the second floor!" the male called after us. "Just swipe the cards to get into your room. Don't lose them or you'll be charged extra!"

We took a primitive vertical transport to the second floor. A long, bland corridor awaited us, leading to even blander rooms. At least I wouldn't have to listen to Cyle's snoring. The walls on our ship were way too thin, as I'd quickly discovered.

A menu with a list of food items lay on a table, but I wasn't hungry. I also hadn't asked Cyle if the food here was palatable for us. I simply took off my C-suit and went to bed, hoping the Intergalactic Authority wasn't on the way to arrest us for breaking dozens of laws by landing on Peritus.

Tomorrow, we'd know for sure if we'd finally found mates and with them, hope for the survival of all Albyans.

4

Jenny

I was early and so were the foreigners. Not that they looked very foreign. Their size was the only thing that set them apart – well, and their kilts. All three of them wore one. I wondered if...

No. I dragged my gaze away from their crotches and focused on the rest of them. They all had ginger hair, even more fiery than my own. Two of the men seemed to be brothers, looking almost identical, while the other had blue rather than emerald eyes. I realised the colour of their kilts matched their eyes. Was that just a coincidence? Here in Scotland, a tartan represented a specific clan. Was that the same for them? Were they from two different clans or maybe families?

I had so many questions. The main one: Were all of them this gorgeous?

The reception area felt very crowded with these three massive males squeezed into it. Steff looked tiny behind her desk, staring at the men with wide eyes. I couldn't fault her for it. I had to press my lips together to stop myself from drooling.

"Hi," I said and suddenly, I was the focus of attention. All three of them stared at me as if they'd never seen a woman before. I looked down at myself. Was there a stain on my blouse? I'd come dressed in my most elegant professional outfit, wanting to impress. My ivory blouse showed a tiny bit of cleavage, highlighting my curves without being too tight. My skirt was about the same length as their kilts and yes, it had a muted tartan pattern on it. I suppressed a groan. I was basically dressed like them. Their shirts were white, almost the same as my blouse. My skirt may not have been as colourful but...

"Come on in, sorry for making you wait."

Pam rescued me as she opened her office door. Her eyes widened when she took in her visitors. Steff chuckled under her breath and I shot her a grin. Seemed like we weren't the only ones affected.

She stumbled back, giving the men the chance to squeeze into her office. Yesterday it had seemed like a large, airy room. Today, it was the opposite. The chairs seemed too small for the foreigners and I was scared they might collapse beneath them.

"Sh-shall I make some tea? Or coffee?" Steff asked.

"Tea," the men said as one.

"With a drop of milk," the one with the blue kilt added, seeming strangely proud of his words. Huh. Weird. His foreign accent was barely noticeable and I probably wouldn't have realised he wasn't from Glasgow if I'd met him on the street. Strange how they had Scottish accents even though they were from abroad.

"And you?" Steff asked me.

"Same. Thanks."

Pam had taken a seat behind her desk, putting some safe distance between her and the males. I didn't have that option. I pulled the remaining empty chair a bit further away from them, not because I was scared or intimidated but because I didn't trust myself not to drool all over them. I'd never reacted to a man in this way, not since swooning over Leonardo DiCaprio as a teenager. It was embarrassing. Silly. Immature. And definitely not professional.

I realised I'd never even introduced myself. Time to catch up on formalities and hope I hadn't made a bad impression.

"I'm Jenny MacPherson, owner of the Publicity Puffin marketing agency," I said so quickly that my tongue almost didn't keep up. "I'm helping Pam with a campaign to get more women to sign up. She told me about your cooperation with her yesterday and I'm really excited to hear more about what you've got planned. Do you have your own marketing team?"

Silence met my words.

"Marketing?" the largest of them asked, seemingly confused. His hair was braided more elaborately than I'd ever managed it with my own hair.

His brother elbowed him in the ribs and I couldn't suppress a smile. That was exactly how Ewan and I interacted. I had no more doubt that they were siblings.

"We don't. We've not needed any advertising because we have so many males desperate to find their mates."

"Mates?" Pam repeated. "Is that what you call it at your agency? I love it. Makes you think of true love, soul mates, the one. Jenny, maybe we should include that in our campaign."

I nodded and pulled out my notepad, using my cast as a table. Other people may have preferred a laptop or tablet, but I was old-fashioned at times.

"What do you call your females?" Blue-Eyes asked. They'd never introduced themselves.

"We usually say ladies," Pam replied. "Although if we put the Scottish angle on it for the campaign, maybe we should switch to lassies? Jenny, what do you think?"

"Lassies," the largest guy said in a slow way as if he was savouring the word. "I like it."

He looked at me and our eyes met. A fireball erupted between my legs and I squeezed my thighs together before I even realised what I was doing. What the fuck? I blinked and looked away, heat blooming in my cheeks. This wasn't going well. Maybe I was getting my period. Or I was pregnant. I hadn't taken a test in a while. Some nights, when he was very drunk, Jason had refused to use a condom. I couldn't take the pill because I'd developed jaundice the first time I'd tried it. The possibility of being pregnant was there, but I didn't have any other symptoms. This hormonal reaction to the strangers had come out of the blue. Maybe it was nothing.

Luckily, Steff returned with a tray. While she poured tea for all of us, I watched Pam. Her gaze was fixed on the men, roaming over them with barely veiled interest. Had I looked at lusty as her? Maybe I'd been worse. Pam was married. Not that marriage meant that you couldn't appreciate these prime specimens from afar.

I wondered if they were as ripped beneath their clothes as they seemed. Had they intentionally sent their three most beautiful guys to make sure Pam signed the cooperation contract with them? I definitely had to ask if they could be part of the photoshoot. We'd – no, Pam would be inundated with ladies desperate for their own hot Highlander.

"Thank you, lassie," Massive-Muscle said when Steff handed him a cup of tea. I was almost jealous at the smile he gave her.

As soon as I got home, I was going to take a pregnancy test. My hormones were all over the place.

Steff blushed and retreated to the reception area, closing the door behind her.

"How many females will this marketing campaign attract?" Blue-Eyes asked.

"If we go with the kilt angle, hundreds," Pam said.

"Thousands," I muttered under my breath. If they all looked like the three men in this room, Scotland would soon be without women.

"Thousands?" Massive-Muscle's brother echoed. "We would like that very much."

This nickname thing was getting tiresome. "Sorry, but I didn't catch your names?"

Behind their backs, Pam gave me a thumbs up.

"I am so sorry," Blue-Eyes said. "We usually have better manners. My name is Jafar of Clan Feallan, Second Scientist of Albya."

"And I am Cyle of Clan Lannadh, First Scientist of Albya. This is my brother Thorrn."

Thorrn. The big guy with the braided hair was called Thorrn. What a strange name. I wanted to say it out loud, see how it sounded on my tongue.

I noted how Cyle hadn't specified his brother's job title. And why were they scientists? I thought they ran a dating agency.

"Is Albya your town?" Pam asked, taking the words from my mouth.

I couldn't help but notice the quick look the three guys exchanged.

"It's where we're from, yes," Cyle said after a moment's pause. "Jafar and I have developed a new way of matching mates, so while we're scientists at heart, we have now taken on the honour of working with your agency."

Ah, that explained it. Scientists turning their discovery into a business. That wasn't unheard of; lots of people did it.

"Do you meet with your applications or is it all done online?" Pam asked. "And how does your science work? You mentioned it in our earlier conversations, but I'd love some more detail. Maybe we can apply the same methods at my agency."

Cyle smiled. "I'd be happy to introduce you to our approach. Maybe we should use a real-life example for a demonstration? A female on your database and a male from ours?"

"Excellent idea. While we do that, maybe one of you would like to discuss marketing plans with Jenny?"

"Me," Thorrn said immediately. His deep, growly voice made me squirm on my chair again. What the ever-loving fuck was wrong with me?

"Are you-" his brother started, but Thorrn gave him a glare that shut him up. I smirked. Yes, they were exactly like Ewan and me. I bet their childhood had been full of squabbles and healthy competition.

"You can use one of the rooms upstairs," Pam said to me. "The one on the right is fully renovated and has a sofa. Or maybe you'd like to go to a café?"

She winked, barely noticeable. I rolled my eyes at her. I supposed she was used to finding partners for others all day long. It was a habit that she now extended to me. I just had to be careful to remind her that she wasn't supposed to pass on my details to the men's agency. I was going to enjoy my single life for quite a while longer before looking for a replacement for Jason. No, not a replacement. A better model. An upgrade. Maybe in a year or so. Definitely not now.

A sofa upstairs sounded a little too cosy, too intimate. "I know a nice little café around the corner. Let's go there."

Thorrn jumped to his feet. "Lead the way, lass."

I didn't get up. "Please don't call me that. My name is Jenny."

His smile disappeared, his expression turned crestfallen. "I thought that was a synonym for female? Did I misunderstand?"

"I also wouldn't want you to call me 'female'. Maybe that's normal in your culture, but here we prefer to be called by our names."

I wasn't sure why I was being so prickly. It was clear he hadn't meant to belittle me. Ah. That was it. Jason had patronised me from the start. I wasn't going to let another man do that.

He gave me a puppy dog look that turned my insides into mush. "I apologise, Jenny."

"Apology accepted. I realise you're not from here." I turned to Pam. "We'll be back in an hour or so. Is that enough time for you to discuss the mating practices of Scottish haggis?"

Not sure why I said that. I supposed I wanted to lighten the atmosphere.

Pam snorted, while the three men looked at me in confusion.

"What's a haggis?" Jafar asked curiously. "Is that what you call your males?"

I left the room before I erupted into hysterical laughter.

5

Thorrn

I looked at the little chair with doubt. I wasn't sure if it would collapse under my weight as soon as I sat on it. Everything in the eatery Jenny had taken me to was small. Tiny, in fact. I kept my arms close to my body, glad the C-suit already had my lower arms pressed tight against my chest. I couldn't wait to be back on our ship and get out of the suit. I felt like I couldn't breathe properly, but I knew I was imagining that. The C-suit didn't compress my ribcage and Peritus's atmosphere was similar enough to that of Albya that we could breathe without wearing a respirator.

Jenny was already studying the menu. "Aren't you going to sit down?" she asked without looking up.

She was so small. This place suited her. Small and dainty and breakable. I hadn't realised humans were this fragile. It made me doubt whether they'd be good females for us. I had a hard time imagining someone as tiny as Jenny giving birth to an Albyan baby. She'd be torn apart.

I gingerly took a seat, vowing to stay as still as possible. Jenny handed me her menu.

"The cherry tart is excellent here, if you want something to eat."

I scanned the menu, finding nothing that sounded familiar except for tea, although I couldn't be sure their tea was the same we had on Albya. Probably not.

A female approached our table. "Know what you want yet?"

"Tea and a slice of cherry tart," Jenny said.

I put down the menu. "I'll take the same."

The female smiled and made a note on her old-fashioned paper pad. "Tea for two. Lovely. I'll bring it over in a sec."

Silence wallowed between us. I wanted to say something, but didn't know what. All of a sudden, my tongue was glued to the roof of my mouth and my brain had forgotten to form words. This female was doing things to me. I'd been rock hard ever since I'd laid eyes on her. My antenna was itching like crazy, but I couldn't scratch it while I was wearing the C-suit. Another reason to get back to the hotel so I could get out of this sgidding thing.

Jenny cleared her throat. "What's your role at your agency? The other two said they're scientists, but I never caught what you do."

For the first time in my life, I wished I'd followed in my brother's footsteps and taken the academic route. What was I supposed to tell her? That I was one of the top cage fighters on my home planet? That I made money by beating other males unconscious? I didn't think she'd appreciate that.

"I help out my brother," I said, not wanting to lie to her. It was the truth. I was only here because I'd agreed to do Cyle a favour.

"And do you have any experience with marketing? PR? Advertising? Social media?"

"Do you do all of that?" Turning the question back to her was the easiest way to avoid lying.

"Yes. I run my own marketing agency, so I do a little bit of everything. I had an intern last summer, but usually I work alone. One day, I'm going to hire a permanent assistant, but for now, I'm a one-woman show."

I was in awe of her. Her outer appearance was clearly deceiving. Peritan females were so small that I'd assumed they'd stay at home where it was safe, protected by their males. Not that those were any less puny. I'd take out a Peritan male without breaking a sweat. A single punch should do it. It was a miracle their species had survived this long. And they'd even made it to be the dominant predator on their planet. On Albya, we shared that role with the taigeis, small but fearsome beasts roaming the wild hills of the Central Highlands. I'd only ever seen one up close and still had the scar on my calf to show for it. It would take at least four Peritans to successfully catch a taigeis.

"Let's talk strategy," Jenny said, pulling me from my thoughts. "I was planning a social media campaign before Pam told me about the cooperation with your agency, and with a few tweaks, I think we can stick to that plan. We should definitely feature some of you in the videos. Kilts and all."

Her gaze flitted down for a moment before she met my eyes again. A pink blush spread across her cheeks when she realised I knew what she'd been thinking of.

"I'd be happy to show you my kilt," I said, my voice strangely hoarse. "From all sides."

I immediately regretted being so forward, but to my surprise, she didn't scold me like she had before when I'd called her lassie. Instead, she turned even more colourful. Was this some strange mating behaviour? A way to show me that she was interested? I really hoped so. I was certainly interested in her. My antenna had been itching ever since she'd stepped into the other female's office, although I couldn't be sure why. My remaining, crooked antenna had a mind of its own, randomly itching and twitching at unexpected times. It wasn't how they were supposed to work, but it shouldn't surprise me that mine was different. It was permanently damaged. For all I knew, it might give me these irritating sensations for the rest of my life. Or until I had it pulled off during a battle. More likely.

"Do you always wear one?" she asked, not meeting my eyes.

"Yes. Unless I'm swimming or in bed. Then I'm naked."

I didn't think she could get even pinker. It was a beautiful colour even though it clashed with her hair.

"And... underneath..." She cleared her throat. "No. Don't answer that. That's incredibly unprofessional of me. I'm sorry."

"No need to apologise; I'd be happy to tell you. I wear-"

"Watch yourselves, sweeties, the teapot is hot." The waitress sat a tray on the small table. "Let me know if you need anything else."

She left without taking the items off the tray. How rude. I reached for the pot at the same time as Jenny. Our fingers touched and I gasped when my antenna burst into flames. I clutched it to make sure it wasn't really on fire and just feeling like it.

"What's wrong?" Jenny asked with concern. "Did I scratch you?"

I shook my head, unable to form words. I hoped Peritans had the same gesture. My antenna was painfully hot and now the itching sensation was returning, making it even more uncomfortable. Realising she couldn't see my antenna, I lowered my hand, resisting the urge to scratch myself.

I didn't know what the itching meant, but there was no doubt about the heat.

Jenny was my mate.

Sgid. I was looking at my actual mate. The female destined to spend her life with me. The missing part of my soul, to be re-joined with mine in the mating ceremony.

"Are you feeling alright?"

There were no words left in my mind. Emotions were fighting for dominance. And just to make it worse, my cock was almost as painful as my antenna. I couldn't look at Jenny for fear of it becoming too much to bear.

"Fine," I finally managed to get out.

"You don't look fine. Do you want to go back to the others?"

Yes. No. I didn't know. I needed to tell my brother about this, but I also needed to be alone with Jenny.

The thought of seeing her near another male made me clench my fists. I scanned the eating establishment. Only one other table was occupied with two females, both older than Jenny. I relaxed a little. No threats. Nobody would take my mate away from me, at least not this very second. But I'd have to plan for the future. Unless...

"Are you mated?" I burst out.

She looked at me in confusion. "What?"

"Do you have a mate? A life-partner."

"No, not that it's any of your business. And speaking of it, we should really get back to talking about my marketing plans. I have-"

I stopped listening, too focused on the fact that she wasn't mated. Thank the Lady Beyra. I touched my thumb to my index finger to form a circle as a quick prayer of thanks. No male would stand in my way. Now all I had to do was take her home to Albya so we could conduct the ceremony, turning us into bonded mates for all eternity. And with the way my cock strained against the thick fabric of my kilt, it couldn't be soon enough.

"Are you listening?"

"No," I admitted truthfully. I didn't want to lie to my mate. "I was..."

"I think it's better if we head back. This isn't working."

Another burst of heat shot in my antenna, making me flinch. "No. We've not even had tea yet."

The pot and cups still sat on the tray, forgotten along with the strange triangular food Jenny had ordered.

"It would be a waste, you're right," she muttered. "Especially the cherry tart. Go on, try it."

This time, I let her rearrange the table, taking everything off the tray. I didn't want to touch her again. It might drive me over the edge. I'd never felt so out of control of my body. I was a fighter; I knew every singly muscle, every sinew. I'd broken most of my bones over the years, so yes, I was very familiar with those too. I was always in control. I was a predator. Yet now, I was being torn apart, the pieces of me gravitating towards my mate. If I wanted her to hold me together, I had to tell her what was happening.

"I need the relief room," I announced and got up, almost toppling over the tiny chair. "Do you know where it is?"

"Relief room? Ah, the toilets? Over there, behind the curtain."

I hurried in the direction she'd pointed at and breathed in deep when I stepped into a small washroom, barely large enough to turn in. As soon as I'd locked the door, I pulled out my commstick.

It took Cyle a small eternity to answer. "What's wrong?"

"Jenny. It's her."

"Her what? Thorrn, I'm in the middle of a conversation, is this important?"

"Yes. She's my mate."

Silence met my words. Maybe I should have prepared him a little before throwing that statement at him.

"Your mate? How do you know?" He sounded dubious. Not that I blamed him. I would have reacted the same way, or even more so. Cyle had come here believing that human females could be our mates. I'd doubted that from the start, yet here I was, my mate next door.

"My antenna got hot and painful. Just like they used to say. It still hurts now even though I'm no longer in the same room as her."

"Are you sure? You didn't bump it somewhere?"

"Pit air iteig, I'm not an idiot. I know what I'm feeling. It's not just my antenna. I'm...hard. And not the kind of hard I get when I rub myself. It's an entirely different level. I've never felt anything like it."

"You should come back. We need to run tests." He was starting to sound more curious than doubtful. "If she really is your mate, we'll know if my instruments are working. Bring her to the ship. It's easiest to do everything there."

"No way. I haven't told her yet. And how do you think she'll react when she finds out that we aren't Peritan? She'll run away. No, I have to explain to her. Maybe start with the mate bond. Telling her that we're from a different planet can come later."

Cyle sighed. "You're right, even though it's annoying. Come back to the agency. I've got a handheld scanner with me; that will have to be enough for now."

I slid the commstick back into my shirt pocket and stared at the mirror to my left. Sgidding C-suit. I couldn't see my antenna without taking it off, but the room was too small to do so. I'd just have to hope that it wasn't injured in some way. It was still hot but not as much as it had been earlier.

Jenny had poured tea into our cups and was already eating her triangle cake. She gave me a small smile when I retook my seat.

"Feeling better?"

I straightened my shoulders and looked right into her eyes. "We need to talk."

6

Jenny

He was making me nervous. Maybe it had been a mistake coming here with just him. Not that I felt uncomfortable in his presence. On the contrary. Although by now my panties were soaked. Thinking about what he might be hiding beneath his kilt had been the final drop in the ocean. Yes, this water metaphor was extremely appropriate. As soon as I got home, I'd put on a new pair of knickers and take a pregnancy test. Something was wrong with my hormones and I needed it to go back to normal.

As much as I hoped that he wanted to talk about advertising strategies, the intense look he gave me promised something else. I both wanted him to stop looking at me like that and do it for the rest of our lives. Something was sparking in the air between us. This man was dangerous for my sanity and the survival of my panties.

He didn't say anything, but his lips quivered slightly as if he was trying to form words.

"What's the matter?" I asked, my curiosity getting the better of me.

"We... I... my..."

His sudden lack of confidence was adorable in a confusing sort of way. Until now, I hadn't thought that this big, bulky male could be this insecure. His stammering made me want to reach out and pat his hand, but that would have been entirely inappropriate. This was still a business meeting. Kind of. It hadn't felt like one and I doubted we'd ever actually discuss strategy.

"I... we need to talk." He breathed heavily and rubbed his forehead. No, that wasn't quite right. He rubbed the air above his head. Maybe some strange tick? Or was he miming something?

"You already said that," I smiled when he didn't say anything further. "What is it?"

"Maybe we should go somewhere else. It'll be easier to show you."

"Show me?" I repeated. "No, I don't think this is a good idea. We need to get back to the agency soon. You can tell me whatever you need to here."

He sighed, his broad shoulders drooping. "Do you... believe in the stars?"

I cocked my head at him. "The stars? Up in the sky? How could I not believe in them? They're there; it's a fact. Please don't tell me you're a flat-earther or something like that."

"I don't know what that is, but I didn't mean the stars as physical objects. I suppose I'm asking if you believe in fate? In the power of the stars to create connections, influence our destiny?"

"I'm not sure. I guess I like determining my own destiny."

I laughed internally. As if. I'd let Jason control my life. That was much worse than fate meddling with it.

"So do I," Thorrn said in his beautiful deep voice. "Some people believe the stars control our lives, but I see them as guides, to be either followed or ignored. They show a possible path and it is our choice whether to walk on it."

"That's very deep. Why are we talking philosophy?"

He took a deep breath and reached across the table, taking my hands. "Because the stars have led me to you. You are my mate."

I was too surprised to pull back. Had he just said what I thought he'd said? Mate? As in partner? Lover? Husband?

That last thought broke the spell and I ripped my hands from his, jumping up so abruptly that the chair almost toppled over. I grabbed my bag and hurried out of the café before realising we hadn't paid yet. Gritting my teeth, I looked around for the waitress, but she was nowhere to be seen. Great. Just great. I was tempted to leave and let Thorrn settle the bill, but I didn't know if he even had cash on him. I very much doubted this little café would accept whatever his country's currency was.

"Jenny."

I didn't look at him, no matter how alluring his voice was. *You are my mate.* The words echoed in my head.

No fucking way.

I hurriedly rummaged through my bag and slammed a twenty-pound note on the counter. I wasn't going to spend a single minute in this man's company. As soon as the café door closed behind me, I breathed a sigh of relief. With one quick look back to make sure he wasn't following me, I walked away as fast as I could.

I only stopped when my feet were starting to hurt. I wasn't wearing the right shoes for walking long distances. These heels were made to impress, not to hike. I looked around for the nearest street sign. I had no idea where I was. I hadn't cared about where I was going, too keen to get far away from Thorrn. Once again, I threw a quick glance over my shoulder. No sign of him. I was kind of surprised that he hadn't followed me. Maybe this had all been just a bad joke and he hadn't actually meant what he'd said.

Yeah, right. I shouldn't lie to myself. He'd been deadly serious. I may have been bad at choosing men, but I was able to tell apart a male who was joking from one who wasn't.

Now that I wasn't moving, I realised how much everything hurt. My bruises reminded me of my last encounter with a man who'd promised me the stars - at first. No, I wasn't going to make that mistake ever again.

I dialled Pam's number, using the seconds before she picked up to make my decision.

"Jenny?" She sounded slightly breathless.

"Aye. I just wanted to let you know I won't be coming back to the agency today. I need to go home."

"What's wrong?"

Of course, she had to ask difficult questions.

"My arm hurts; I think I need some rest." Not a lie. Not completely.

"You poor wee thing, of course. I should have asked if you were well enough to work."

Guilt rose up in me. I didn't want her to feel bad because of my half-lies. "It's alright, I just forgot my painkillers. I would have been fine otherwise. Can we meet tomorrow and talk about the campaign?"

"Aye, but we can push it back a day if you need more time to recuperate. I was planning to show our new partners the city and-"

"WHERE IS SHE?" Thorrn's voice was so loud I had to hold the phone away from my ear.

He'd returned to the agency rather than follow me. Why did that disappoint me?

"I think Thorrn wants to talk to you," Pam said drily. "Shall I pass the phone to him?"

"No, I need to go. See you tomorrow."

I hung up before she could give Thorrn the chance to grab the phone from her. Before I could even consider my next steps, the phone rang again. My brother's name flashed on the screen. Shouldn't he be at work?

"What's up?"

"Where are you?" His voice was heavy with concern.

"Out. Why?"

"Anna just called. Your ex turned up at the house demanding to see you. She called the police, but he left before they arrived."

Fuck. I didn't know why I'd expected him to stick to his bail conditions. I'd been with Jason for long enough to know that he didn't respect authority, especially not the police. It shouldn't come as a surprise that he'd break bail, but I guessed I'd still believed in the tiny spark of decency inside of him. The part of Jason I'd fallen in love with.

"Are you okay?" Ewan asked.

"Aye. He'll probably go to my office next. Fuck, I need to grab some stuff from there."

"Don't. Come home, take a cab. Anna will still be there for a couple of hours, so at least you won't be alone. I'll try and get off work early."

This is why I loved my brother. He truly cared about me, more than Jason ever had.

"Don't worry," I muttered. "It'll be fine. He'll go to my office, then maybe the pool. I doubt even he is stupid enough to come back to your house."

Ewan chuckled darkly. "Jason is stupid. I know you didn't want to see it, but he's not just a cunt but a fucking foolish cunt. I'll talk to my boss now. I'd feel better if I'm at home with you where I know you're safe."

"Don't. It's fine. I've got my laptop with me; I might sit in a café for a few hours and do some work. He gets bored quickly plus he's lazy, so I bet he'll be back home on the sofa soon."

"Are you sure?"

"Aye. Don't risk giving your boss another aneurism."

He laughed. His boss was a passionate Italian who threw the biggest temper tantrums I'd ever seen. It was only because his heart was as big as his anger that Ewan still worked there.

"Text me when you're on your way home," he said. "Please."

"I will. See you tonight."

I stared at my phone after ending the call. What now? My heart was beating faster than it should. I shouldn't give Jason this power over me, but no matter how brave I'd pretended to be with Ewan, I was scared. My arm was proof of how volatile Jason could be. One broken bone was enough. I wasn't going to let him hurt me any further.

A delicious smell hit my nose and I looked around for its source. A grin spread across my face when I saw where it came from. I put my phone away and hurried towards the waffle house.

7

Thorrn

I didn't hear a single word said. I let Cyle and Jafar do all the talking while in my mind, I went over every moment of my time with Jenny. My mate. My antenna was still itching like crazy. Only my years of training my body stopped me from scratching it constantly. Below my kilt, my cock was hard and erect.

Pam had shot me a few strange looks when I'd come back without Jenny, but thankfully the others distracted her.

I couldn't wait for them to be done. I needed to get back to the ship so we could run tests. I knew Jenny was my mate, but maybe seeing it as a scientific fact would help her understand.

"What do you think, Thorrn?"

I blinked at Jafar who was smirking at me, knowing exactly that I hadn't been listening.

"I think we should continue tomorrow," I said with a glare directed at the scientist. "We might get a new perspective on things."

"Excellent idea," Pam said cheerfully. "I suggest we celebrate signing the contracts. There's a pub around the corner and I'm happy to buy the first round."

That wasn't what I'd intended. Why were humans so sociable?

"I'll go back to the hotel," I announced. "You do what you want."

I didn't even try to be polite. My itching antenna was driving me crazy, as was my cock, still hard and pushing against my C-suit. As soon as I was back on the ship, I'd be able to do something about that. The thought of jerking off to her image made me even more aroused. Pit air iteig. I was behaving like a youngling during his first heat.

I left before they could say anything. I had to get to the ship's lab and find out what was going on. I didn't know much about science and wasn't able to run the tests my brother would be able to do, but even I could operate the medpod. Hopefully, it would tell me if my antenna was itching that way because I'd found my mate.

Not that I had any doubt about it. Jenny was my mine. She'd realise that soon enough.

I decided to walk rather than take one of the human transportations known as taxis. I had to clear my head. It took me a while to realise that I was walking much faster than the Peritans around me. I slowed my step just a little to avoid being stared at. I didn't want my brother to chide me for drawing unwanted attention.

"Nice kilt!" someone shouted, but I ignored them. Humans seemed to be obsessed with our traditional dress, even though I'd seen at least two Peritans with the same checkered kilt. I wasn't sure if their designs signified their clans like ours did, but I didn't care enough to find out.

When I turned a corner, my antenna suddenly grew hot. I stopped in my tracks and wrapped my hand around it. Together with the itching, it was painful enough to make me cringe. I was tempted to simply rip it off. It was clearly damaged beyond repair. Maybe I could ask Cyle to remove it surgically once we were back on the ship. I knew Jenny was my mate, which meant I no longer needed my crazy antenna.

That's when my antenna moved. It jerked to the left, pressing against my hand. It had never done that before. What was it going to do next? Climb off my head and dance on the street? Sgid. I winced and tightened my grip on it. Again, it pushed to the left. A suspicion grew at the back of my mind. I was standing at a crossroads and had intended to turn right, heading towards the airfield. Did it want me to go left? Was there something it wanted to show me?

It was ridiculous. My antenna didn't have independent thought. But doubt made me cross the street. What would it hurt to follow the sgidding thing's directions? I was curious. Pit air iteig. Now I was following the whims of a broken appendage. Cyle would be laughing at me - not that he'd ever find out. I was going to keep this to myself. He and his perfect antenna didn't know what it was like. I'd always pretended to be fine with the loss, but it had been hard. Still was. I wasn't complete. Without my mating antenna, I was only half a male, unattractive and unable to find a mate.

Until Jenny.

Curiosity spurred me on and I hurried in the direction the still hot antenna was leading me. I kept a hand wrapped around it so I wouldn't miss any movements, even if that looked strange to the Peritans passing me. With my C-suit hiding my antenna, to them it would seem like I randomly held up a fist above my head. Not that I cared.

Left, right, straight on, right again. After five clicks of following my antenna's direction, I was starting to feel silly. Maybe those were just involuntary jerks that meant nothing. It had led me into a quiet residential street with only a few Peritans mulling about. I couldn't see anything of interest. Houses, vehicles, a few pitiful-looking trees. Birds chattering on the roofs above me was the only sound. Nothing that would warrant my attention.

I was about to turn back when a scream shattered the silence. The sound made a shudder run down my back. I knew that voice. Jenny.

I ran towards the scream, dreading what I might find. She'd sounded terrified.

In the distance, a figure was being pulled into a large vehicle. Jenny was being taken in front of my eyes, but I was too far away still to help her.

"Jenny!" I shouted, running faster than ever before. The door was pushed shut behind her and the vehicle took off with screeching wheels. They were taking my mate.

I wouldn't let that happen.

While running after the vehicle, I pulled out my commstick, fumbling until I found the pilot's contact entry.

"I need you to take off and come to my location," I screamed into the commstick as soon as he answered. "Now."

Vaxx spluttered something inaudible, but he must have realised the urgency of the situation. "On my way. I'm going to keep the chameleon shields engaged."

Stating the obvious. Not that I would have cared if he'd landed our ship in the middle of the city square, not if it helped Jenny.

I was just about able to match the vehicle's speed, but I couldn't keep this up for long. They were getting faster, probably aware that I was following them. Vaxx had to get here fast. I could have tracked the ship on my commstick, but that would have made me slower and I couldn't afford to be distracted.

My muscles started to ache. I was used to strength training, not endurance. Fights didn't take long once I got in the ring. I wasn't one to play with my opponents. I simply knocked them out as soon as I got the chance. Now, I wished I'd done more endurance training. I was getting out of breath. Running with my secondary arms restrained made me a tiny bit off balance.

With every click that passed, the white vehicle got further away from me. We'd entered a busier part of the city and it kept getting harder to avoid other vehicles and Peritans crossing the street. Shouts followed me, but I ignored everything. I only had one mission. Save Jenny. Nothing else mattered.

My commstick beeped. "Almost there," Vaxx's voice crackled. "I can see you now. I take it you're pursuing that white rolling craft?"

"Yes. Stop it but don't shoot it. My mate's inside."

"Your..." He was silent for a moment. "I'll do whatever I can. You can stop running now; I've got a hold on it."

Before my eyes, the vehicle started to slow down while shaking from side to side. I hoped Jenny was safely secured so she didn't get hurt. The only people who'd get hurt today were those who'd abducted my mate.

Suddenly, the vehicle vanished. Vaxx must have extended the chameleon shield to hide it from Peritan eyes.

"I'll send you coordinates where I'll land," he told me through the commstick. "I've got the vehicle secured and will keep it locked until you arrive."

A map appeared on the device with a blinking dot not far from my location. Thank Lady Beyra. My ribs hurt and I was having trouble breathing. Not to mention the pain in my legs and feet. I couldn't wait to get out of the C-suit to stretch out and extend my secondary arms. Having them pressed against my ribcage restricted my breathing more than I'd realised.

Still, I didn't slow my pace until I reached a small green space. A metal bench was bent at one end, giving me an indication where Vaxx had parked the ship. I ran to the bench and the ship appeared as soon as I stepped into the chameleon field. Next to the ship was the vehicle. Someone was banging against the metal doors from the inside.

"Need help?" Vaxx asked.

"No. I'll deal with this myself." I put away the commstick, freeing up my hands. I was going to kill whoever had abducted Jenny.

The driver's seat of the vehicle was empty. Vaxx had said that he'd locked the doors, so they still had to be inside. The large sliding door Jenny had been pulled through was closed. I grabbed the handle and took one deep breath. I was scared of what I might find. It was a strange sensation. I was never scared. I didn't like this cold, clammy feeling at all.

With one forceful pull, I ripped the door off the vehicle, flinging it to the side. Three humans stared at me, two with fear and shock, one with surprise. Jenny was flanked by two males, her hands bound with rope, a piece of cloth tied around her neck. The front of it was wet; they must have used it to gag her. Fury boiled up in me.

"Are you hurt?" I growled, ignoring the males for now.

She shook her head, but she was shaking all over. I reached out and pulled her from the vehicle. The males made no attempt to stop me. Good. Not that it would save them.

I pressed her against my chest, breathing in her scent. Mate. My antenna stopped burning and I only now realised that it had been hot the entire time. The itching reduced to a gentle tingling that almost felt pleasant.

"Are you hurt?" I repeated, this time as a whisper. I rubbed my cheek against hers. Her skin was so soft.

"I'm fine," she muttered. "My wrists are sore, but that's just because of the rope. You can let go of me now."

Never. I was going to hold her for the rest of my life. Never let her go. She'd almost been taken from me. I couldn't let that happen again.

"Mine," I whispered, my voice hoarse. "Safe."

"You'd make a great caveman." A small laugh tumbled from her pink lips. How could she laugh after what she'd been through? My mate was stronger than I'd thought. Pride at her resilience filled me. Other females would cower in fear, traumatised, but not my Jenny.

A sound behind her made me turn just in time to see one of the males climb out of the vehicle. I almost laughed at his desperate escape attempt. He wouldn't get far. Even if I didn't pursue him, Vaxx likely had a lock on him. He'd shoot him before he left the confines of the chameleon shield.

"Who are they?" I asked Jenny before letting go of her. Just for a moment, just until I'd killed her kidnappers. Then she'd be in my arms again.

"One of them is my ex. I don't know the other."

"Ex?"

"He was my boyfriend until I left him."

Boyfriend. I didn't like that word at all. A former mate. When I'd asked her at the eating place, she'd told me she was unmated. She hadn't mentioned this *ex*.

I grabbed the one trying to escape with one hand while dragging the other out of the vehicle with the other. They struggled, but they were weak. I lifted them by their necks until their legs dangled above the ground. They squirmed and squealed like prey. Disgusting.

"We didn't mean it!" the pale-haired one whimpered. "I just wanted to bring Jenny home. She's my girlfriend. She-"

"Girlfriend," I roared. "You call her your friend, but you harmed her. You took her against her will. I will make you pay for injuring my mate."

"Don't hurt them," Jenny pleaded.

I turned to her in surprise. "They harmed you."

"They tried to, but they didn't succeed. And yes, Jason broke my arm and-"

I roared with fury. I hadn't realised someone had caused my mate's injuries. I'd assumed she'd been in an accident, not the victim of a male's aggression. It made me even angrier. I may have let him live for kidnapping her. Maimed, mutilated, but alive. But he'd broken her bones. Caused her pain. That was unforgivable. I looked into their eyes, searching for any sign of regret. Only fear stared back at me. The acrid odour of urine reached my nose. One of them had pissed himself. I despised them. They had no honour. They deserved no honourable death.

"She's mine," the *ex* spat, giving me a defiant look.

There was no holding back. Without thinking, I snapped both males' necks - regretted it immediately. That had been too quick. I shook their corpses, willing them to return to life so I could kill them all over again.

Jenny screamed and I stopped shaking them for a moment. She stared at me in shock, her eyes wide.

"You killed them," she whispered.

"I did. They hurt you."

There wasn't more to say about the matter. A male who hurt a female didn't deserve to live. That was the law. Once, before the Sleep, there had been other rules. Males would have been put to trial. Now, females were so precious that harming them was an automatic death sentence that could be carried out by anyone who witnessed the crime. I wasn't a murderer. I was an executioner.

I let the bodies fall to the ground before picking up Jenny. She squealed and tried to wriggle her way from my grasp, but there was no way I'd let her go.

My crooked antenna tingled with approval as I carried my squirming mate into the ship.

Jenny

I was on a spaceship and I hadn't even noticed. Too much had happened. First, Jason appeared out of nowhere. He'd just wanted to talk - until a white van pulled up behind him and I'd found myself kidnapped. I hadn't been scared that he might kill me. Jason was a bully, but he wasn't a murderer. I expected him to drive me back to his place and keep me there, but instead, the van had started shaking as if it was about to turn over. Jason and his driver had screamed and tried to regain control while I simply watched, frozen in shock.

For some reason, I hadn't been entirely surprised when Thorn had torn open the door of the van. I should have been, but I wasn't. I couldn't explain that strange intuition. Just like I couldn't explain my new surroundings.

We stood - and with that I meant that Thorrn was standing while I was wrapped in his arms, my feet dangling high above the floor - in a hangar filled with large metal crates and strange robotic machines. Some of them moved, others were silent witnesses. Even if I could have believed that all this technology was built by humans, I couldn't explain away the alien walking towards us.

Four arms. A kilt. Just as tall as Thorrn. Reddish curls framed his face. And on his forehead, two grey antennae. They were sleek stalks with a round bulb at the ends. And did I mention the four arms? The top pair was where arms should be, but a second pair, slightly smaller, grew just underneath. The antennae could have been part of an elaborate costume, but the arms were definitely alien.

I should have been shocked, scared, maybe even fainted. Instead, I simply stared at the alien. He stared back.

"Vaxx," Thorrn greeted the male. "This is Jenny, my mate."

The alien stared a while longer, then touched his forehead with his right hand. "Welcome to the *Epona*. Thorrn, you are truly blessed. Have you confirmed the match yet?"

"No, but I intend to do so now. Take us back to the airfield. I don't want to stay here a click longer than necessary."

"What did you do with the males?" Vaxx asked.

"They're no longer a threat," Thorrn grumbled, his voice dark. It should have sent me off screaming, but instead, I felt a strange warmth inside my chest. He'd eliminated the threat to me. And killed two men. I really shouldn't feel good about that. Was it too late to run?

The heavy doors behind us slid closed, shutting out the sunshine. Definitely too late.

"I'll take care of their bodies," Vaxx said and disappeared up a flight of stairs, leaving me alone with Thorrn.

"Let go of me," I demanded.

"No," he growled, tightening his grip on me.

I kicked at him, hoping I'd hit his crotch, but no such luck.

"I won't run," I tried. "I just want to stand on my own two feet."

"No."

He buried his head in my hair and breathed in deep. Was he sniffing me? Weirdo.

Time to use my only remaining weapon.

"My arm hurts. You're hurting me."

That did it. He gently set me down and took a step back, but kept his hands on my arms as if he couldn't bear not to touch me.

"You should have said," he muttered. "Is it the existing injury, or did they harm you further?"

"I think I banged my cast against the walls of the van. I should probably get it x-rayed again just in case. And would you please remove those ropes?"

I held out my hands to him, still bound. I hadn't even realised; the pain from my wrist had been overshadowing the discomfort the rope had caused.

Guilt flashed across Thorrn's face and he quickly undid the knots. I sighed in relief when the rope fell to the floor. I stretched out my arms and rolled my shoulders. "Much better. Now can you let me out of this place so I can get to a doctor?"

He shook his head, his expression growing wild again. "No."

"You can't keep me here forever."

"I can. You're my mate."

We were going in circles. How could I get through to this caveman who seemed to have bathed in testosterone?

Without warning, he picked me up again, this time swinging me into his arms until I hung there like a baby, his arms beneath my knees and my arms. He'd moved so fast, I hadn't even been able to make a sound of protest.

"Are you an alien, too?" I blurted. Deep inside, I already knew the answer, but I had to hear him say it.

"You're the alien." He looked down at me and smiled. It was such a transformation from the feral, angry man who'd killed my ex that I wanted to rub my eyes to make sure I was really seeing this.

"Are you here to invade Earth?"

Thorrn chuckled. "No, we're here to steal all the women."

I gulped. "You're joking, right?"

"Of course I am. There's only *one* female I intend to steal. But let's get you to a medpod. Peritan medicine is barbaric. I cannot believe your healers can't even mend a broken bone yet."

"Peritan?"

"Earth's intergalactic name is Peritus. Humans are Peritans," he explained as if that made any sense at all. "I've been wondering why Peritans don't know that."

"Maybe because we've not had any aliens come and tell us?" I deadpanned. "Now drop me. I can walk by myself."

Instead of an answer, he crossed the hangar so fast that I would have had to run to keep up with him. We stepped into a round lift big enough for at least ten people. Maybe six if they were all the size of Thorrn. The walls were the colour of white gold, polished and shimmering. As soon as the elevator doors closed behind us, screens appeared on the golden surface, showing all sorts of writing that didn't make sense to me. The symbols looked a tiny bit like Celtic knots, but that may have just been my brain desperately wanting to match my alien surroundings with something familiar.

Thorrn held his hand against the wall and alien language appeared around his fingers. He tapped some of the symbols and the lift started moving upwards. As a little experiment and to show Thorrn that it was better if he stopped holding me like a baby, I pressed my foot against the golden screen. Nothing happened.

He chuckled. "It only responds to Albyans."

I dimly remembered Jafar saying he was a scientist of Albya. Pam had asked whether that was his town, but now I had a different suspicion.

"Is Albya your planet?" I asked.

"It is. And it's going to be your home once we finally leave Peritus."

"My...my home?" I spluttered. "No way. I'm not coming with you. You're... an alien."

"I told you, you're the alien here," he said, seemingly unconcerned as if he had no doubts that I'd be staying with him. So arrogant. And very, very wrong. I'd get off this ship before they left to wherever their planet was.

With a slight shudder, the lift came to a stop and the doors slid open soundlessly. I'd expected a futuristic looking corridor, but instead, Thorrn walked us into a massive circular room. Glass partitions created smaller rooms around the edge, while in the centre of the room were five large seats, their backs to each other, forming a pentagon.

Thorrn pointed at one of the rooms of the glass donut. I almost giggled when I realised that it really did look like a donut cut into slices. "That's one of the medpods. To the right of it is Jafar's lab, followed by my brother's. I'll give you the full tour later, but first, we need to fix your arm."

He carried me to the room he'd pointed out. It didn't have a door, but when he pressed his hand against the milky glass, an opening appeared as if by magic. It was just big enough for him to squeeze us through. My blouse caught on an edge and was pulled up, exposing my side.

Thorrn sucked in a breath. "What happened to you? I didn't realise Peritans have mottled skin."

I pulled the blouse back down. "Just a bruise. Nothing to worry about."

His brows pulled together, but he didn't comment further. Instead, he finally set me back on my feet. "Don't move," he commanded.

I wanted to give him some kind of snarky retort, but that's when the floor of the empty room split apart and a jacuzzi rose from underneath.

It was oval, maybe three metres long, and inside, dark blue water bubbled soundlessly. I couldn't see the bottom of the pod and now that I was taking a closer look, it didn't seem like it was water after all. It was a gooey substance that threw up bubbles at the surface without drops or steam above it.

"Nanites," Thorrn explained. "They will analyse your injuries and fix them."

"I have to go into that? Is it safe for humans?"

"It's compatible with any species known to the AI." He frowned. "Maybe I should check if that includes Peritans."

I took a step away from the medpod. "Please do. I don't fancy being turned into soup."

Thorrn pressed his hand against the wall and just like in the lift, alien writing appeared all around his fingers. He made a fist and the golden writing left the wall, now floating in the air. Wow. It looked like magic, even though I knew it was advanced technology. Thorrn wasn't a wizard.

"It's safe," he confirmed after a while. "You need to take off your garments."

"You want me to strip in front of you?"

From the grin on his face, he had no issue with that whatsoever. "If you don't disrobe, the nanites will get confused. They might think it's part of your skin and attach the clothes permanently."

Alright, he had me convinced.

"Turn around," I told him firmly.

"Why? You're my mate."

I sighed. We were back to that. "I'm not. You need to get that out of your head. I'm not going to get naked with a stranger in the room, a man at that. Turn. Around."

His grin had disappeared and the sad puppy eyes he gave me now made me want to reach out and pat his head. He really believed that we were mates, whatever that meant. But almost being abducted by my ex had taught me one thing: being single was exactly what I needed. No more deceitful guys who were nice at the beginning, only to show their true nature once it was too late. Thorrn may seem like a good guy, if a little strange, but I wasn't going to make the same mistake again. From now on, I was going to keep men at arm's distance. Maybe the occasional one-night-stand to satisfy the physical urges, but that was it.

Thorrn was still looking at me as if I'd kicked him.

"Turn around or I won't go in there," I repeated one last time. To my relief, he finally did as I'd asked and looked at the door instead - the door that was no longer there. The opening had closed without me noticing. Would it open if I wanted to leave or was I trapped, reliant on Thorrn to let me out?

The throbbing pain in my arm reminded me that there was a bigger issue to deal with first. With a quick glance at Thorrn to make sure he wasn't peeking, I slipped out of my clothes as fast as I could. I suppressed a wince when I accidentally touched some of the larger bruises. This medpod better do what Thorrn had promised.

"What do I do with my cast?" I asked. "I can't take it off. It needs to be cut off if you want me to remove it."

"Don't worry," he said without turning around. "I can tell the nanites to dissolve the cast."

"Without dissolving my hand?"

He chuckled. "Trust me."

I gingerly touched the bubbling goo with one finger. It was warm and soft. I sniffed my finger. That was reassuring. With a deep breath, I climbed into the pod. The blue substance lapped against my legs, not at all uncomfortable.

"Can I look now?" Thorrn asked and I quickly lowered myself until only my head poked out.

"Yes. What happens next?"

Thorrn wiggled his fingers and the golden symbols rearranged. "I will activate the nanites. For me, it always feels like I'm being tickled, but it might be different for you. It won't hurt, though, I give you my word."

I believed him. Let's hope he was right.

"You will have to submerge your head for just a click so the nanites can analyse if there's any damage," he said. "If you're lucky, they won't remove your hair."

"My hair?" I squeaked, ready to jump out of the medpod. I probably would have if I hadn't been naked.

Thorrn laughed, his emerald eyes blazing with mirth. "I'm joking."

"You evil... alien."

His grin widened. "You don't know the half of it."

Why did that turn me on like nothing else?

"Submerge your head," he ordered. "Before the nanites get bored."

Somehow, I didn't think that was possible, but what did I know about alien technology? I'd read about nanites in science fiction novels, but I didn't even know if us humans had already managed to create them. I certainly hadn't imagined them to look like blue, bubbling goo.

I held my breath and let myself fall backwards. The nanites didn't give way like water would have. Instead, they gently lowered me into their depths. Bubbles pushed against my back like a soothing massage. I could get used to it.

I stayed submerged for as long as I could, then broke the surface, gasping for air.

"Well done," Thorrn said. I could hear the smile in his voice even though my back was turned to him. "Your hair is still intact. I could ask the nanites to change its colour, if you wish?"

"No," I snapped, sounding harsher than intended. I loved my hair, but I hadn't always. At school, I'd been bullied for having bright ginger hair. Together with what my mother called elfin features, I'd been told that I looked otherworldly and - in the words of my classmates - ugly as fuck. It had taken me years to not only like, but love the in-your-face colour of my hair.

"Just joking. I wouldn't change your mane even if you asked me to. We match perfectly. Our offspring will be blessed."

Offspring. He really was deluded. Maybe I should stop humouring him and try to escape. There had to be a way off the spaceship.

A strange ethereal sound that made me think of angels ringing tiny bells made me turn to look at Thorrn. On the wall next to him, more golden text had appeared along with graphs and charts. And a stylised image of my naked body. Great. It wasn't just a generic outline of a human body. No, I recognised the features. It even showed the mole I had beneath my right breast and the scar on my palm from the power drill accident.

Thorrn stared at the image. I was glad I couldn't see his expression.

Another bell sound and bruises appeared. I looked down at my arm and compared them. The nanites had scanned me perfectly, showing exactly where I'd been injured.

"I wish I could kill him again," Thorrn growled. "I want to rip him apart. Slowly. Then I'll have the nanites stitch him together so I can start over, again and again, until..." He sighed deeply. "I'm so sorry I wasn't there to protect you."

He turned to me and the guilt painted across his gorgeous face took me aback. Did he really feel guilty for something that wasn't his fault in the slightest?

"The only person at fault is Jason," I said softly. "I don't need anyone to protect me. I should have walked out sooner, but it wasn't my fault either. It was Jason who hit me."

My brother would be proud. He'd corrected me every time I'd blamed myself for Jason's abuse. I almost believed it. Almost.

Thorrn's expression didn't change. "I should have found you sooner. My brother has been talking about going to Peritus for ages. I could have been here many Albyan rotations ago. I could have protected you. But I didn't listen to him. I didn't think..."

"Didn't think what?" I asked when he didn't continue.

"Didn't think that I'd ever find a mate."

"Why not? You're..." I stopped myself before I could tell him just how sexy I thought he was. "I bet if your profile was in Pam's database, dozens of women would be interested in you. Scratch that, every single one of them."

Thorrn ran his hand over the air above his head. "No. I'm broken. I didn't think I'd find a mate because I'm broken."

My skin was starting to tingle while the bubbling around me increased, but I didn't want to mention it to Thorrn, not while he was baring his soul.

"I don't understand," I said softly. "How are you broken?"

He sighed, once again rubbing the space above him as if he was touching something invisible. Maybe he was. It wouldn't be the strangest thing I'd seen today.

"It's easiest if I show you."

He touched the button at the collar of his shirt and it started to glow. Just like the rest of him. His entire body lit up, glowing brighter than a lightbulb. I had to avert my eyes and when I looked at him again a few seconds later, Thorrn had changed.

Massively.

He now looked like the alien I'd seen earlier. He'd sprouted two extra arms and a single, small antenna on his forehead. That had to be what he'd rubbed while talking to me.

His chest seemed even broader, but that may have been because his shirt had disappeared. Now he was wearing nothing but the kilt. His shoulders and upper arms were covered in dark tattoos that curled around his biceps, highlighting his defined muscles. The patterns seemed familiar, like some sort of Celtic design. If you'd ignored the second set of arms and the slightly bent antenna, he could have still passed as human.

Until the tattoos started to glow green, the same colour as his kilt. Alright then. Definitely not human.

"See? I'm broken." He pointed at his antenna. I didn't quite understand what he was on about. Surely he didn't think he was *broken* just because he didn't have two perfectly formed antennae like the other alien, Vaxx? Was he really that vain? I hadn't put him down as someone obsessed about their appearance, but it wouldn't be the first time I'd been wrong about a man.

I didn't know what to say. Was I supposed to tell him that I didn't care about a broken antenna? That might give him the wrong idea. I didn't want him to think that I was interested in him. Because I wasn't. Definitely not. I was happily single and didn't need a four-armed-sexy-guy-with-a-kilt-and-whatever-he-might-have-underneath. Wait, if he had double arms, did that mean he had double down there, too?

I realised I was staring at his kilt and quickly turned away from him to hide my blush.

That's when the nanites started to boil.

9

Thorrn

S he couldn't even stand the sight of me. She turned away, unable to look at my damaged body. I shouldn't be surprised. If the females on Albya were awake, they'd turn in disgust as well. A male was nothing without his mating antennae. How else was he supposed to find his mate? While females had antennae, too, they were smaller and didn't have the same reach. They only helped to confirm the match, but the females couldn't use them to find their male from afar.

Jenny had no antennae at all. She wasn't able to feel that we were mates. Or could she?

Suddenly, she screamed. At the same time, an alarm bellowed from the speakers above. The lights began to flicker. Something was very wrong.

"Get me out of here!" Jenny yelled. I didn't even think. I simply dragged her out of the medpod and wrapped all four arms around her, protecting my mate from whatever was hurting her. The nanites in the pod rose in strange tendrils as if searching for her. Some of the healing substance was still on her skin and it seemed to hurt her. Jenny whimpered, clearly in pain.

"It's alright," I muttered even though it wasn't. Nanites weren't supposed to behave like that. I'd never seen a medpod malfunction.

I grabbed her discarded clothes and used them to rub her body, trying to get all the remaining nanites off her skin. I avoided looking at Jenny's face. I knew she was crying and seeing those tears would only make the pain in my heart worse. She'd got hurt in my presence, again. I hadn't protected her.

I was a failure.

"What's going on?" Vaxx asked through the intercom. "I'm getting all sorts of error messages. It looks like an electrical fault near the lab."

"Get Cyle!" I shouted. "My mate is hurt!"

My brother would know how to help. No way was I going to put her back in a medpod. I wasn't going to risk it.

"Changing course. I'll notify him. We'll be at his location in three clicks."

That was three clicks too long. Jenny was still whimpering, trying to rub her arms, but too weak to do it properly. I carried her out of the room, away from that sgidding pod, and gently lowered her to the floor. Maybe the cold metal would soothe her pain.

"Where does it hurt?" I asked, even though I was sure of her answer.

"Everywhere," she whispered. "It burns."

Pit air iteig! How could the nanites that were supposed to heal her do this? Her bruises had disappeared, leaving her skin soft and pale, but at what cost?

I continued rubbing her skin with her clothes. Most of the blue colour had faded, but from the way she was still in pain, the nanites were clearly still there. I needed a scanner, but I couldn't leave her alone, not even to run to the lab. I wasn't a scientist or healer; I had no clue what I was looking for. I needed Cyle.

How long had it been since Vaxx had changed course? One click? Two?

Her clothes were soaked. I needed towels, but the nearest fabricator was too far away.

I ripped off my kilt and unfolded it. Jenny had other worries than seeing me bare before our mating ceremony. She may not even be aware of that tradition. While I steadied her with my lower set of arms, I gently rubbed the cloth over her skin with the upper pair.

She moaned and I wanted to moan along with her. I may not have been in physical pain, but my soul was writhing in agony. I felt so helpless. What kind of male was I when I couldn't even ease her pain?

The doors slid open and Cyle and Jafar burst in. My brother was by my side in an instant, already pulling out his medscanner. I sometimes teased him because he never went anywhere without it, but now I couldn't have been more grateful.

"What happened?" he asked while scanning my mate from top to toe.

"I put her in the medpod. Everything was normal, but then she started screaming and the diagnostics showed all sorts of nonsensical data. The nanites seem to cause her great pain, but I don't know why. I tried to rub it all off, but..."

"You can't rub them off," he said without taking his eyes off his scanner. "But I can reprogramme them to conglomerate in one spot."

"Then do it."

"I'll get the tools," Jafar said from behind us and hurried off.

"Thorrn?" Jenny whispered. Her saying my name in such a pain-stricken voice hurt me more than any punch I'd ever received in the ring. I hadn't known I could feel like this. I was in pain because she was in pain.

"I'm here." I stroked a strand of wet hair from her forehead. I wanted to lean down and kiss her, but it felt wrong to do so without her permission. Not now while she was vulnerable. "You're going to be fine."

She looked up at me, her eyes brimming with tears. I wasn't sure if she could even see me clearly in her current state. Her lips moved, but no sound came out.

"What are you trying to say?" I whispered, turning my head so her lips almost touched my ear. But it was too late. Her eyes fluttered shut.

"What's happening?" I shouted at my brother. "Is she dying?"

He didn't look up from his tools. He'd attached a cuff to her wrist which would give him more data than his scanner. "No, I've given her a sedative. She's going to sleep while we deal with the nanites."

My throat choked up. "Thank you."

Jafar came running and handed Cyle a small tool not unlike the scanner. "I've already set it up. You just have to choose where the nanites should collect."

"It needs to be skin," Cyle said thoughtfully. "But with so many corrupted nanites in one spot, it will likely leave a burn mark. Brother, do you want to decide for her?"

Without thinking, I took her hand in two of mine. "Transfer them to me."

Cyle gave me a sharp look. "Are you sure? They might be even more painful for an Albyan."

"I'm sure. Just get them off her."

My brother nodded. "As you wish. I'll try and make it quick."

I gripped her hand tightly, waiting for the pain. It was the least I could do.

She looked so pale, so vulnerable. Not at all like the confident female I'd talked to only a few IG hours ago. Her skin was red and blotchy all over, competing with the fiery colour of her hair. I was glad she was no longer conscious.

Cyle's instrument beeped and a fraction of a click later, my upper right wrist was on fire. Not literally. I looked down at it, but there was nothing to be seen. I grit my teeth, trying very hard not to scream. If this was the pain she'd felt all over her body...

I was never going to forgive myself for putting her in the medpod without waiting for Cyle to make sure that it was safe. I'd been cocky and now she was paying the price for it.

"Not much longer," my brother said and pointed his scanner at me. "It's burning through the outer layers of your epidermis. It will definitely leave a mark. I'm sorry."

"I don't care," I growled. "Is she going to be alright?"

"I need to run more tests to find out just how much damage the nanites caused. It will be easier once we know why they behaved as they did. I'll contact the Medical Council to see if anyone else has ever had this happen. Medpods are supposed to be foolproof."

He didn't have to say that he thought I was the fool. He and every single Albyan male were desperate to find their mates. I had a mate, yet I'd damaged her. It was unforgivable.

"It might be best to return to Albya," Jafar suggested. I'd forgotten the male was still here. "It will be easier to run tests on her there."

"Tests?" I echoed.

He looked at me as if I was an imbecile. "She's the first female mate we've found since the Sleep. Of course, we're going to have to study her. She might be the key to finding more mates."

An image of Jenny tied to a lab table flashed through my mind.

"Ton air eigh dhut!" I snapped, glad my mother wasn't alive anymore to hear me use such language. "You will not experiment on my mate. If you put your filthy hands on her, I will cut them off myself."

If I hadn't been holding Jenny's hand, I'd have launched myself at the scientist. No one was going to touch my mate.

"You know I'm right," Jafar growled back. "I'm not the only one who wants to study her. Just ask your brother."

I looked at Cyle who had the decency to look guilty. "Just some basic tests and diagnostics," he muttered. " No experiments. Nothing that would harm her. I'm sure once she finds out about the Sleep, she'd be happy to help..."

The betrayal was almost as bad as the pain in my wrist. It was getting worse. I had to force myself not to squash Jenny's by accident. I hadn't felt such agony in a long time. It was worse than all my ring injuries put together.

In an effort to calm myself, I stroked my mate's hair. Her curls reminded me of the shoots of the Xangi tree. As children, we'd broken off the shoots to play with. They turned hard once they were off the tree and could be used for all sorts of silly games. My pet canine had loved to gnaw on them.

"Almost done," Cyle announced without meeting my eyes. "Three... two... one... that's all of the nanites. You can let go of her hand. Follow me to the medpod."

I hated leaving Jenny's side even just for a click, but I had to get rid of this pain to properly look after her. I got to my feet and faced Jafar. "Leave."

He looked like he was about to argue, but he made the right decision and hurried away. He was a puny scientist who'd likely never had a fight in his life. I could have killed him without breaking a sweat.

"The medpod, quickly," my brother reminded me. "We need to get the nanites there before I lose control of them. We don't want them to spread."

I followed him to the malfunctioning medpod. It was no longer bubbling inside, which in itself was a bad sign. Once I found out who was responsible for its failure, I'd make them suffer. Nobody hurt my mate without repercussions.

"What now?" I asked.

"Hold your hand just above the surface, but don't touch it."

I held my wrist with two of my other hands to make sure I didn't touch the blue goo. I didn't want to find out what would happen if I did.

Cyle did something with his device, it beeped again, and then my pain was gone. I took a deep breath and rotated my wrist, amazed at how I'd gone from agony to zero pain in an instant. But Cyle had been right. It had left a mark. A strange circle was burned into the inside of my wrist, wobbly and uneven as if a child had drawn it. If that was the only negative result of this entire episode, I wouldn't complain.

"Can I go back to her?" I asked. As soon as he nodded, I hurried back to Jenny. Her breathing was more even now, but her skin's discolouration was worrying.

"Usually, I'd like to put her in a medpod," Cyle said, following me. "But under the circumstances, we'll have to treat her the old-fashioned way. I'll keep her sedated while I work on her burns and any other injuries she may have sustained."

"How long will it take?"

"Hard to say. I don't know enough about Peritan physiology to give you an accurate estimate. But I may not be able to wake her up until we reach Albya."

"Does that mean we're leaving?" I asked in surprise.

"I'd like to stay one more day to discuss details with Pam at the agency. Now that we know Albyans and Peritans are compatible, I want her to start recruiting females. It's probably time to tell her that we aren't Peritans – or do you think we should keep that secret for now?"

I looked down at Jenny, who'd taken the fact that I was from a different planet surprisingly well. Maybe Peritus was ready to take its place in the galaxy.

"Tell her," I said. "Then Pam can decide whether to tell the females or not. She knows her species best."

"Agreed. Jafar, Vaxx and I can do the filming with her tomorrow so you can stay with your mate. Then we'll go home. We can organise everything else via the quantnet." He gave me a small smile. "Let's get your mate in a more comfortable position."

I nodded. "And then I'm going to find out who hurt her."

They wouldn't breathe for much longer.

10

Thorrn

C av glared at me. If we'd been in the same room, I doubt we'd still be standing. We'd be on the floor, my fist around his throat, my foot on his balls.

"You will surrender her to us," he repeated for the third time. His voice could have cut through Lavian steel. But he couldn't intimidate me. He was just a scientist and unlike my brother, he had no muscle to speak of. He'd be helpless in a fight. I couldn't take him seriously with his perfectly white lab coat and ring-covered antennae. It was the latest trend on Albya among the upper class. Cav's rings were made of the most precious metals to flaunt his wealth. One of those rings could have fed a family for several rotations.

He hadn't become the clan elder responsible for science and health because he was particularly qualified. He'd bought that role, everybody knew it, but his family was too powerful for anyone to speak up.

"How do you even know about her?" I growled. We were only halfway on our journey back home. My brother had promised that he would wait to tell the clan elders about Jenny in person. I certainly hadn't told them. That left Jafar and Vaxx.

Our pilot was a good male, a friend of Cyle's, and I trusted him. Jafar, however, was different altogether. He was ambitious, too much so, and he hungered for recognition. As long as my brother was First Scientist, Jafar had no way to progress in his career.

"Jafar," I answered my own question and looked around for the male. He'd been in the central comms room with me earlier, but had made himself scarce. It would only give him a reprieve of the pain and suffering I'd cause him.

"Did you know he's my cousin's eldest son?" Cav grinned. "I'm blessed to have such a loyal family." He turned serious again, his glare returning. "We will wait for you at the spaceport. You will give her to us."

"I will not. She's my mate and if you try to even lay a single finger on her, I will kill you."

"Are you too stupid to see what this means?" Cav asked. "This changes everything. She might be the key to finding a cure to the Sleep. If she holds the answer, we can wake our females. We won't have to look for mates among inferior species."

"Peritans aren't inferior," Cyle interjected, speaking up for the first time. "They may not be as physically strong or technologically advanced, but they're resourceful and intelligent. My brother's mate isn't a lab animal to be studied and experimented on. She's a female, the first non-Albyan mate, and we need to treat her as the precious miracle that she is."

I shot him a grateful look. It took a lot for Cyle to stand up to his superior. He wasn't like me. Wasn't a fighter.

"We don't need Peritan mates," Cav snarled. "We have our own females who can bear us Albyan offspring. We don't even know if we can breed with Peritans."

I balled all four of my fists. This male had it coming. As soon as we reached Albya, I'd seek him out and treat him like he wanted to treat my mate. I turned my gaze to the screen at the bottom left. Jenny was sleeping, looking peaceful and serene. Her skin was slowly turning less red, but she still hadn't recovered completely. I spent most of my days sitting by her bed, watching her sleep. Not being able to do anything was awful. I brushed her hair, I washed her, I wet her eyes and lips so they wouldn't get too dry. I ran muscle stimulisers over her arms and legs to make sure she wasn't going to be too weak to move once she woke. And I talked to her. Told her about Albya, about my family. I told her things I'd never spoken of aloud. I bared my soul to her. I both hoped and feared that she'd remember what I'd said once she woke up.

Cyle ran daily tests on her, both to monitor her health and to learn more about her species. I allowed those tests as long as they weren't more invasive than a blood sample. I understood the gravity of the situation. I wasn't an idiot. We needed to make sure we could find mates for the rest of the Albyan males, or our kind would go extinct. But Cyle understood that as my mate, I couldn't let any harm come to Jenny.

There would be no experiments.

I'd kill anyone who tried.

"We will await you at the spaceport," Cav snapped, clearly angered by the fact that I wasn't paying him any attention. "With a large number of security personnel. If we have to subdue you, we will. With pleasure."

He ended the transmission and I sank back in my chair.

"I won't let him take her," I told Cyle. "I'll die before I give her up."

"I know," he said soothingly. "I will talk to the other clan elders. Maybe they will see reason and overrule Cav."

"And if they don't?"

Cyle sighed. "Then we can return to Earth where the two of you are safe."

I'd been desperate to leave that planet in order to be with my mate, but now, it might end up being our home. I didn't care. As long as I was with Jenny, I was alright with living anywhere in the universe.

I got up and flexed my arms. "I'm going to deal with Jafar."

I signed the agreement with a flourish. My brother set his signature beside mine and handed the commtab back to Elder Havn. The male smiled and nodded in approval.

"Thank you, this was the right choice."

I tried very hard not to glare at him. "It wasn't like we had many options."

Havn lowered his voice. "I know. I'm sorry. The council was divided. This was the best deal I could get for you."

I forced a smile. "I appreciate your help."

He stepped back and turned to the crowd. Half of Priomh, the capital city, seemed to have come to the spaceport to see the first female mated to an Albyan in a generation. Not that they got to see anything. Jenny was in a secure hospital pod that we'd move to my house as soon as we got out of the port. All the spectators got to gaze at were Vaxx, Cyle and me. Jafar was still on the ship, hiding his bruised face. He could have gone into a medpod to heal the injuries I'd inflicted on him, but he was scared. Vaxx had figured out what had caused the nanites to malfunction – an electrical fault that had sent a power surge through the computer that programmed the nanites – but all of us were wary of the pods. Cyle had promised to claim compensation for Jenny from the manufacturers.

Cav appeared next to Havn, fixing me with a familiar glare. My brother put a hand on my shoulder as if I needed him to hold me back. Perhaps I did. My blood was boiling at the sight of Cav, but attacking him now would destroy the truce we'd created. The agreement was the best solution Cyle had been able to negotiate. Jenny had a week to recover and to get used to being on Albya, then she'd take part in tests run under my brother's supervision. There would be nothing done without her consent. Nothing that would hurt her. And I was allowed to be with her.

I wasn't happy about it, but it was necessary to protect my mate from Cav and his friends. Cyle was going to choose the scientists and healers to join his team. He'd report not just to Cav, but to the entire clan council. And as soon as more Peritan mates were found or the

Albyan females were woken from the Sleep, all experiments would stop.

Jenny and I would be able to live in peace.

I turned away from the crowd and went back on the ship to get my mate.

11

Jenny

Jason followed me into my dreams, tormenting me, doing worse things to me than he had in real life. He hurt me. He laughed at me. Yet every time he thought he'd won, a four-armed alien would appear to save me. He'd whisk me away in his spaceship and we'd live happily ever after.

I was strangely aware that I was sleeping, but I couldn't control my dreams. I had to watch as Jason belittled me, broke my bones, took my dignity. Without Thorrn, I would have gone insane. But he was there, every time. Sometimes, he killed Jason. Other times, he only hurt him. I didn't know which I preferred. I was growing numb to all the violence.

When I finally woke from my dreams, I wasn't surprised at all to look into green eyes. Thorrn's face was inches above mine. If I'd had the strength, I could have pushed off my pillow to kiss him. But my body felt heavy as if a weighted blanket was covering me from top to toe. Even my eyelids were heavy.

"Jenny," he breathed.

Kiss me.

"Is she awake?" Someone else appeared in my field of vision, a male much older than Thorrn. He wore a strange visor over his eyes; an alien equivalent of glasses?

"She is," Thorrn confirmed and stood up straight. "Finally."

The other alien smiled, but somehow it didn't feel sincere. Maybe that was because I couldn't see his eyes. "Good. I'll give her a booster shot, then you two can have some time alone to catch up. I'm sure your female has a lot of questions."

I didn't like how he called me Thorrn's female. I was my own person, thank you very much. Thorrn rescuing me again and again didn't change that.

The male touched my wrist, but I was too weak to sit up to see what he was doing. I just had to trust him and Thorrn. Not something that came easy to me.

My wrist suddenly started feeling really cold, as if it had been dunked in ice water. I was about to complain when the cold dissipated. A wave of energy passed through me and I instantly felt stronger. Not strong enough to get up and walk, but at least I didn't feel as if I was about to pass out again.

As soon as the other male had left, Thorrn leaned closer. "How are you feeling? Are you in pain?"

I did a quick mental body scan. No pain. Only heaviness and a remaining sense of weakness. That I could deal with.

"No," I said – no, croaked.

Thorrn held a straw to my lips and I sucked, trusting him. That surprised me. Or maybe it shouldn't. After dream upon dream of him saving me from harm, it wasn't strange for me to trust him. I had to remember that those had been dreams, not reality. To be fair, he'd also rescued me in real life, but then he'd kidnapped me and brought me onto his spaceship.

"Are we still on your ship?" I asked after drinking the tasteless liquid he offered.

"No, we're at my home. We got here three IG days ago, but Cyle didn't want to wake you until he was sure your body could cope with our atmosphere and gravity."

"Wait..." Vertigo overcame me and I had to close my eyes. "We're..."

"On my planet, yes," he said gently. "I had to bring you here for treatment."

I almost scoffed. I bet that wasn't the only reason, just his excuse. He'd never intended to let me stay on Earth, not with this whole I'm-your-mate-thing. For now, I'd let it go. I had more important questions I needed answers to.

"What happened? I remember the burning. I felt like I was on fire."

"An electrical fault," Thorrn explained. "A power surge confused the nanites, changing their programming. Instead of healing you, they attacked you. We're lucky that not all of them were affected. While some of them tried to dissolve your skin, others were healing you at the same time. We managed to remove them, but it was unsafe to put you into a medpod again. We didn't know how the nanites would react. My brother treated you throughout the flight and then the healers here on Albyan did the rest."

"How long?"

"How long you were sedated? In your time, I think it equates to five Peritan weeks."

I'd been out for over a month. I'd been away from Earth for over a month. My brother had to believe I was missing. He'd be searching for me. Maybe he thought Jason had killed me. Or had they found Jason's body? That would have worried him even more.

"Pam informed your family," Thorrn said as if he'd read my mind.

"Wait, she told my brother that I'd been abducted by aliens?"

Thorrn chuckled. "Not quite. I believe she said that you fell in love with a very handsome male and followed him to a meditation retreat on a remote island with no access to communication. You should probably message him soon."

"Ewan would never believe that."

He laughed again. "Pam can be very persuasive when she wants to be. Apparently, she's been sending him postcards in your name. I doubt he'll be surprised when you tell him that you're going to stay with your extremely good-looking male for the rest of your life."

Arrogant, much? That was the second time that he'd pointed out his looks. During our last conversation, just before all hell had broken loose, he'd been miserable because of his broken antenna. Now he seemed to think he was some kind of Adonis. What had changed?

"How do I contact him?" I asked. "If we're on another planet, won't there be some kind of delay? He'd notice that."

"Not when using the quantnet. My brother has supplied Pam with quantnet access, so we can route the call via her."

"I have no idea what you're talking about."

He gave me a grin. "Don't make me explain the technology because I have no idea how it works. I just know that it'll let you talk to people on Peritus."

I returned his smile. "Fair enough."

For a moment, we sat in silence. Not because I didn't know what to talk about. I had so many questions - but which one to start with?

"Is there still something wrong with me?" I asked eventually.

"No, your body has been healed. Your skin may still be a little sensitive, so you will have to use some protective cream before going outside, but otherwise, everything is back to how it should be. You're not weak because you're ill, but because your body used up a lot of its resources in the healing process. I was told you may be hungrier than usual, so I shall provide you with food whenever you want." His eyes widened slightly. "Are you hungry now? Should I get you something?"

I laughed. "I'm fine, don't worry. Am I allowed to leave the bed?"

Not that anyone could stop me. I needed to know where I am. But it felt nice to at least ask and pretend to be happy about being here. In truth, I didn't know what to feel. I was on a different planet, far away from home, far away from my family, but at the same time... I was on an alien planet! Probably the first human to ever set foot on this planet, or any planet that wasn't Earth.

Trying to find a way to get straight home felt like a wasted opportunity.

"Under supervision," Thorrn said, not looking very happy about it. If he could, he would have probably made me stay in bed for the rest of my life, just so I could be with him as his *mate*. He was such a caveman.

"Then show me your home."

I sat up as much as I could with the heavy blanket weighing me down. My vision went blurry for a moment, but returned to normal once I'd sat upright for a moment. Something beeped to my right and I realised a screen attached to the bed was showing my vitals. At least I assumed that's what all the scribbles, graphs and moving lines were. A cuff was wrapped around my wrist. It was so light that I hadn't even noticed it until now.

"Keep that on," Thorrn told me. "It'll monitor your wellbeing."

"I don't think I want to be monitored."

He didn't look happy at all. Caveman appearing in three... two... one...

"Please," he muttered. "I need to know you're alright."

I couldn't resist the puppy dog look he gave me.

I sighed. "Alright. I'll keep it on today. But tomorrow, no more monitoring."

"Agreed - if part of the bargain is that I get to carry you."

There he was, the caveman.

"I can walk," I protested. I wasn't actually sure if I was strong enough to walk unaided, but I'd find out soon enough. I didn't want him to carry me like a child. Or prey. With him, it was more likely the latter. Despite the way he was mothering me, I couldn't forget how he'd snapped Jason's neck as if it was nothing. He was a predator, an alien way stronger than a human. He had four arms, four very large, very muscular arms with hands big enough to crush skulls. Or cup my arse. Heat rose to my cheeks. And into other parts of my body. I couldn't believe I was still horny. It was as if nothing had happened, as if I was still in that cafe on Earth, pressing my thighs together to stop myself from squirming on the chair. This man was going to be my downfall.

"Is everything alright?" he asked, a frown pulling his bushy brows together. "Shall I call a healer?"

I shook my head. "I'm fine. Why are you asking?"

"You changed colour."

"I'm just... I'm too warm; it's the blanket."

To my relief, he bought that little white lie and swiftly pulled the blanket off me, revealing that I was wearing nothing but a simple white gown barely reaching to my knees.

He also used it as the excuse to lift me into his arms. His lower set of arms, that was. His right upper hand steadied my head.

"I'm not a baby," I seethed. "Set me down right now."

"It was our deal." He grinned. "You accepted."

"I didn't. I can walk. Stop treating me like I'm a child."

He looked at me in genuine confusion. "You're not a child. If you were a child, I'd carry you on my back. Only females get carried like this."

Words failed me. He made it sound like his kind regularly carried their women in their arms. What kind of planet had I ended up on? Did this mean women had no rights?

"Why do you insist on doing this?" I asked, trying very hard not to scream at him, punch him or claw at his chest. "I have two legs. I can walk."

"I like the way it feels when your skin touches mine. It makes me feel...more."

"More?"

He shrugged, amazingly only using his upper arms for the gesture, meaning I stayed in place. "I assume it's the mating bond. I have asked the clan elders if the things I feel for you are normal. They only laughed and told me to spend time with you instead of bothering them."

I hesitated before asking my next question. I wasn't quite sure I wanted to know the answer. "What do you feel? For me?"

He straightened and looked away from me. "You wanted to see my home. Let me give you the tour."

This man was infuriating. He needed a kick in the balls. I wasn't a violent person, but maybe that would shock him into behaving. All I wanted was for him to not carry me, not talk about mating and to answer all my questions. That wasn't so hard, right?

"Tell me," I insisted.

He rubbed his crooked antenna, still not looking down at me. "I feel more than I ever have. I'm a warrior, a fighter. I'm not an emotional male. I'm also not a poet. I don't have the words to describe it."

"You don't have to be a poet to talk about your feelings."

He scoffed. "You're wrong. Only females and poets are good at that."

"Is that so?" I couldn't hide a grin. "Then maybe you should take some poetry lessons."

He looked aghast. "I told you, I'm a warrior. It would be shameful to be seen engaging in such frivolous pastimes. The other fighters wouldn't take me seriously. They already make fun of my missing mating antenna, but now that I have you, they will learn to be respectful. I'm the first Albyan since the Sleep to have found a mate. My brother and the other scientists confirmed it."

I sighed. Here we were again. It was time to change the topic.

"Do you have a kitchen? I think I'm hungry after all."

12

Jenny

His house reminded me of the spaceship. It had a large round common room in the centre, with other rooms arranged around it in a circle. A donut of rooms with lots of free space in the middle. The roof was a dome of shimmering glass. It was all one continuous piece of glass, no joints or seams in sight, which made it very obvious that this house wasn't on Earth. Above us, a large sun shone high in the sky. It was maybe twice as big as the sun I was used to and I thought I could almost see it move. I didn't know much about physics, so maybe it really was faster than ours, or this planet rotated faster? I had no idea.

"Is it safe for me outside? Can I breathe the air?"

Thorrn nodded. "The scientists have reassured me that the atmosphere is similar to your Peritan air. Gravity is different, so you may feel a little lighter when you move. Be careful not to jump until you're used to it."

"I wasn't planning on playing hopscotch."

"Hop-what?"

"It's a children's game where you jump across squares."

Thorrn grinned. "And here I thought you weren't a child."

I glared at him. "Stop twisting my words and give me food."

He'd sat me down on a floating dick-shaped sofa in the centre of the room. Other people would have called it oval, but right now, the heat between my legs was messing with my brain. Thorrn carrying me around had been too much for my poor ovaries to bear. His warmth, his scent, his touch... I hoped he didn't know the effect he had on me. After I'd had some food, I'd ask for a shower. I needed lots of cold water to get rid of the urge to jump him.

"Would you like some taigeis?" he asked while waiting for a machine to fill two glasses.

"What's that?"

"A local delicacy. Taigeis are small yet fierce animals that are fiendishly difficult to catch. A friend of mine, Eron, is one of the few Albyans who've ever managed to tame them. He runs the only taigeis farm and charges high prices for his meat, but as a friend, I get a discount."

He pulled a rectangular slice of glass from a pocket hidden somewhere in his kilt. Writing appeared on it, the same knot-like scribbles I'd seen on the spaceship.

"This is a Commstick," Thorrn explained and sat down next to me. His thigh touched mine. "I'll get you one later. It's how we communicate with each other."

"Like a smartphone?"

"Yes, although that's like comparing a wooden cart with a stellar-class space cruiser."

He swiped across the glass, pressed some symbols, then a holographic image appeared above it. A cute, round, fluffy animal looked at me, its tiny nose twitching. It reminded me of a large hedgehog except that I was sure its chestnut fur would be super soft, not spikey. On its forehead were two pink antennae, miniature versions of those Albyans sported.

"This is a taigeis," Thorrn said and stroked the hologram with one large finger. The animal leaned into his touch as if it was alive and here, not just a simulation. Wow, this technology was really way more advanced than ours.

I reached out to touch it, but my hand found only air - until I accidentally brushed against Thorrn's finger. I stilled as a sudden heat exploded across my skin. This had to be what menopause felt like. Hot flushes all over.

He captured my hand and brought it to his lips. I should have pulled back. Should have...

He pressed a kiss to my knuckles. The way he looked at me... as if I was a meal he wanted to devour.

My mind went blank. All strength of will left me. His eyes bored into mine and I felt like I was about to burst into fire. Not the painful fire I'd felt in the nanite pool. No, this was the kind of searing heat that would pull me out of reality and into a realm of bliss like I'd never experienced.

He didn't let go of my hand. He kissed me again, and again, and again, working his way up my arm. Tingles spread across my skin in a web of desire. I wanted him. So much. Needed him.

And why was I holding back? What would it hurt to give in? Just the one time. Maybe that would quench the urge and everything would go back to normal.

Just once.

"Kiss me already," I whispered.

His eyes widened ever so slightly, then I was on his lap, two sets of arms holding me tight. He waited for a split-second as if giving me one last chance to turn back, then his lips were on mine, hard yet soft. I let go of all doubts.

Just this once.

I opened to him, letting him claim my mouth. His kiss was wild and untamed. Two of his hands cupped my cheeks while his other pair gripped my hips, pushing my pelvis against him. Something hard waited beneath his kilt. Would he look like a human male?

His tongue swirled against mine and a moan broke from my throat. That only spurned him on further. He fisted my hair, holding me in place. His teeth nipped my bottom lip and for some reason, that turned me on like nothing else. I wanted him to bite me. I'd never felt that desire before. What on Earth was happening to me?

He slid up my gown as much as he could while keeping me firmly pressed onto his lap. When his hands cupped my arse, I couldn't help but moan again. He squeezed, pushing me forwards against his hardness. Only his kilt separated me from his cock.

How I wanted him. I needed him to take me. The kiss was no longer enough. I was burning with need and he was the only one who could douse the flames.

I ground against him. That should be a clear message, right?

Thorrn groaned, squeezing my cheeks.

"My mate," he breathed in between kisses.

For the first time, I didn't mind him calling me that. In fact, I wanted him to say it again. Whisper it in his husky voice like it was the most precious word in the universe.

I couldn't resist any longer. I reached down and squeezed my hand under his kilt.

He froze. I opened my eyes to see him look at me with a strange, tortured expression.

"I can't," he muttered. His lips were red and swollen; I bet my own looked just the same. His antenna, usually crooked, was erect, standing straight and proud.

"What's the problem?" I whispered. I didn't want to ruin the moment with loud words, but it felt like it was already too late.

"We have to wait. I can't claim you until we're mated."

I blinked, not quite understanding what was happening. He wanted to wait?!

He moved his hands from my arse, leaving me feeling strangely bereft. An hour ago, I hadn't planned to even kiss him and now, I was painfully disappointed that he hadn't gone beyond that.

"Why?" I asked. I sounded embarrassingly needy.

"It's tradition. We have to do the handfasting ritual before I can claim you properly."

"No sex before marriage? Is that what you're saying?"

He nodded solemnly.

Just how old-fashioned was this planet? What had I got myself into?

"I'm sorry," he said. I believed he was. If the bulge beneath his kilt was anything to go by, he wanted this just as much as I did.

I climbed off his lap and straightened my gown. My hair was all over the place and my skin felt flushed all over, but there wasn't much I could do about that. I took one of the glasses he'd put on the table earlier and busied myself with tasting the clear liquid. It had more taste than water should have, a vaguely flowery flavour. I took slow sips while deciding on my next move.

"Does that mean you've never had sex?" I asked eventually.

He looked slightly affronted. "I have had intercourse. With males. But I have not engaged in *mating* with a female. I was waiting for my mate - and if I hadn't found you, I'd stayed celibate. We no longer have females on Albyan."

"Woah, what did you just say? There are no women?" And he had sex with guys? But I didn't voice that question.

Thorrn sighed. "I was hoping to delay this discussion."

"You can't say something like that and then refuse to explain."

"You're right." He sighed again. "It happened a few days after I had been formally recognised as an adult. After the ceremony, my mother had been more tired than usual, but we thought nothing of it. My father, the First Scientist at the time, made her lie down and rest. The next morning, she stayed in bed. And the day after. Until she didn't wake up."

His voice was heavy with sadness. I took his closest hand, wordlessly encouraging him to continue.

"She wasn't the only one. The sickness spread so fast that we didn't even have a name for it when the last female fell asleep. Every adult female was trapped in an endless sleep that they could not be woken from. The healers and scientists tried everything. My father spent day and night in his lab, desperate to find a cure. But nothing worked. The females stayed asleep and every female who reached maturity succumbed to the Sleep as well. With our technology, we were able to keep them alive, but they never woke up."

"That's awful," I muttered. "And they're still asleep even now?"

Thorrn nodded. "The ones who're still alive. It was quickly noticed that whenever a male died, his mated female would also perish. It made males more cautious. They were now not only responsible for their own life, but also for that of their mates. But old age can't be cheated. Now, only the females who were young or unmated are still alive. There are facilities across the planet where they're cared for. My father tried to find a cure until the day he died, taking my mother with him."

I pulled him into a hug. My throat was tight with sadness at what he and his family had gone through.

"How did he die?" I asked softly.

"An accident. A fire at his laboratory. He tried to get my mother out, but he was trapped by the flames. Then there was an explosion..." He shook his head. "It was a long time ago. My brother took up our father's mantle and has been dedicating his life to finding either a cure or new mates for us. And I... well, I didn't."

He turned away from me. "I didn't think it was possible. I was stuck in the belief that we were destined to go extinct as a species. And so I lived in the moment. If I'd known that you were out there... that hope wasn't lost..."

I cupped his face and forced him to look at me. "How could you have known? Don't blame yourself."

Thorrn smiled sadly. "Of course, I blame myself. I could have been with you many rotations ago. I wasted so much time on fighting, drinking, throwing my life away. I should have been searching for you." He reached out and gently stroked my cheek. "I'm sorry your mate is an idiot."

"Think of it like this, if you'd turned up on Earth a few years ago, I wouldn't have been single. I wouldn't have been working for the dating agency and we would never have met."

Slowly, he nodded. "You are right. The stars brought us together at just the right time. I just wish..."

"What?"

He untangled himself from me and got to his feet. His expression was hard to read. Embarrassment? Guilt? Sadness? A mix of all three?

"I need to tell you something. Please don't hate me."

A cold shiver ran down my back. This couldn't be good.

13

Jenny

"You did what?" I screamed. "I'm not a lab rat! I won't do it!"

He reached out, but I pushed him away, stumbling backwards. The pain on his face almost lessened my anger, but then his words echoed in my mind and I held onto my fury.

"I want to go home," I snarled. "Now. You can't do this to me."

"I'm not doing anything to you!" he shouted before clasping a hand over his mouth. "I'm sorry," he said quietly. "I fought for you. They wanted to take you away as soon as we landed. My brother and I managed to change their minds. You're not going to be a lab...rat, as you call it. I'm going to be there the entire time. They won't hurt you. I swear."

His shoulders were slumped, his expression sad and beaten. It was hard being angry at him when he looked so defeated.

"You fought for me?" I asked, breathing hard.

"I did. You're my mate. I'm always going to fight for you. I'm going to protect you no matter what."

An image flashed into my mind, Thorrn holding Jason and his accomplice, shaking them, fury etched across his face.

I no longer pitied Jason.

And I was glad Thorrn had been there.

And that he was here now.

My anger dissipated, swept away in an instant. "You'll be there?" I whispered.

"I won't leave your side. And if they try to hurt you, I'm going to kill them."

There was no doubt in my mind that he would really do so. I'd seen him break a man's neck without hesitation. He'd do it again if he had to.

It should have scared me. Instead, I felt safe with him.

I sat down again, exhausted from my outburst. Thorrn went on his knees in front of me, as if he didn't dare join me on the floating sofa.

"If you don't want to, we'll find a way," he promised. "We can go back to Peritus."

My eyes widened as I took in what he'd just said. "You're offering to take me home?"

"If that's what you want. If it means you're safe and happy."

"But..." I didn't know what to say. I knew how much it meant to him to be here among his people. And how important it was for Albyans to find a cure for the Sleep. I couldn't even imagine what they'd been through. I didn't know how old Thorrn was, but if the females had been asleep since he'd been an adolescent, we were talking decades. Two, at the very least. A planet full of Sleeping Beauties.

"I'll do it," I said, decision made. "I want to help. I don't like how it came about and how nobody actually asked me, but I can see how you need me. Not just you but your planet." I snorted. "That sounds ridiculous and very, very self-obsessed."

Thorrn took my hands, his eyes full of emotion. "Thank you. You don't know what this means to me."

"How long will it take? The tests?"

"I don't know. Cyle is very meticulous and he'll probably want to run every test at least twice. He's always been like that. Once, when we were younglings, he corrected our educator in front of the entire class. He ended up having to go to the institute's director to explain himself. Cyle wasn't nervous at all. He made a long list of all the educator's shortcomings and-"

"I've heard this story before," I interrupted him. "How do I know this? How do I know that Cyle wasn't punished but put into a more advanced class?"

Thorrn's eyes widened. "I told you while you were asleep. Cyle wasn't sure if you'd be able to hear me, but I wanted you to know that you weren't alone."

Was it possible for a heart to explode in one's chest? Mine certainly felt like it was close to doing that. A wave of emotion swept over me and for a moment, I couldn't form words. I choked up.

"Are you alright?" he asked softly. "Do you need to rest?"

I shook my head. "I've never felt better." An image sprang to my mind. "You and your brother had a pet. I don't know what kind of animal it was, but you said how you competed for its affection. Your brother read books about its species, but you sat next to its enclosure for days until it trusted you."

His eyes lit up. "Yes. Little Artair. I miss him. He lived long beyond his natural lifespan, which was probably due to my brother giving him all sorts of potions. Our parents never found out how Artair lived as long as he did."

I chuckled. "You and Cyle were close."

"Aye, we were. Talking about our childhood made me realise that I want us to become close again. When the Sleep began, we drifted apart, but now we have a chance to change that. As much as I hate you being subjected to tests, it does mean that we can spend more time together as a family."

I squeezed his hand. "You're such a softie."

He raised his eyebrows in shock. "Soft? Me?"

"You've got a hard shell but I'm starting to think that you're very sweet inside. Like a lychee."

"I have no idea what you're talking about. I'm a fighter. A warrior. I'm not... *sweet*."

I laughed. "Yes, you are."

His thumbs rubbed my palms and tingles broke across my skin again. I was still horny. That was the only word that fit. Horny, needy, desperate.

"So... no sex before marriage? That's the rule?"

I'd never been this forward. With Jason, sex had become a chore, something he wanted and I had to give. I couldn't remember the last time I'd instigated it. Maybe at the very beginning of our relationship, but even then, he'd been the one setting the pace.

I barely recognised myself. My hormones had to be all over the place.

But it wasn't just a physical need. I *liked* Thorrn. Even though we'd met not long ago, I felt like I knew him. He'd been in my dreams, every single one. Somehow, I didn't believe that it had all been my subconscious. I was sure he'd been there in some strange way, guiding me through the darkness of my memories. When I looked at him, snippets of information popped into my mind, the things he liked, what he'd done in the past. Maybe my brain had been injured – or maybe he'd talked to me while I was asleep. I kind of liked that thought. Him sitting by my bedside, talking, spending time with me.

Now, he was offering me a new life and I'd be a fool not to consider it as an option.

Going back was easy. Taking the first step on a new path was a challenge I was ready to attempt.

Thorrn groaned and squeezed my hands. "I'd love nothing more than claim you right here, right now. If things were different, I might do just that. But you're the *first*. I want to do things properly."

But did I want that? Right now, I wanted sex. I was a little embarrassed to even admit that to myself, but a girl had needs. I wanted him on a physical level. But was I ready for more? I'd only just woken up on a different planet, for goodness sake. While technically,

I'd found out that Thorrn was an alien five weeks ago, to me it felt like yesterday. I was still processing the fact that aliens even existed. And now I was sitting next to one, holding his hands.

Did I like him? Yes. Despite his caveman manners, I liked him.

"I think you need some time to think," Thorrn said softly and got up. He stroked my hair and I found myself leaning into his touch. Yet more proof how much my body wanted him. "I will prepare the food I've been promising you for too long. You must be starving."

He was so considerate, so thoughtful. When I'd first met him, I would have never guessed he had such a gentle side to him. He was the complete opposite of Jason. My ex was soft on the outside and hard inside. Rotten, even. Thorrn had a hard shell, but the more I got to see of what he was hiding beyond that rough exterior, the more I liked him.

And that was the problem. I shouldn't even consider being with him. I had family on Earth. I had a job. A life. I couldn't just throw it all away for a man I barely knew - or could I? Maybe it was time to take risks. Staying with Jason had been the easy route. I hadn't left when I should have. I hadn't been able to take that step. But the one thing he'd taught me was that I deserved better. I deserved more. I wanted a partner who truly cared for me, who loved me no matter what, who looked out for me when things got bad, who always had my back. Thorrn was such a man. There was no doubt in my mind. I felt like I *knew* him. It had to be due to all the things he told me while I'd been unconscious. And that mysterious mating bond.

I was no longer going to pretend I hadn't felt it from the moment I'd laid eyes on him. The physical reaction had been instant. If what he said was true, we were meant for each other. Destined by the stars. I wasn't religious. I didn't believe in a deity or higher power. But there was no denying that I felt connected to Thorrn in a way I'd never felt with anyone else.

The stars have led me to you. That's what Thorrn had said. Maybe I was overthinking this. My gut told me that he was right for me. That this wasn't just about physical attraction. It was so much more.

Should I listen to my brain or my heart, my instinct? My head was starting to hurt. This wasn't a right or wrong question. There was no simple answer.

Maybe I should wait. I didn't have to do this now. I could control my urges, no matter how much my core throbbed and ached for him. I wasn't some wanton hussy.

But... I didn't want to wait. I wanted him. Now.

I opened my eyes. I hadn't even realised I'd closed them. I'd made my decision. Suddenly, everything seemed clearer, brighter.

"Thorrn," I called out. He was by my side in an instant, balancing two bowls in his lower hands.

"Yes, my mate?"

I smiled at him. "Tell me what we need to do to make this official."

Thorrn

She wanted to become my mate. I felt like rubbing my eyes and cleaning my ears. Moments ago, she'd been screaming at me. Now she was ready to be claimed as mine. Did all females change their moods and minds this quickly? I would have asked my father, but he was no longer there to give me mating advice. My brother had never had a mate, either, even though he was a few rotations older.

I'd have to figure it out on my own.

"There are two stages to the mating ceremony," I said slowly. I watched her every move, every twitch of her facial muscles to make sure she really wanted this. It was a dream come true and I couldn't wait to make her mine, but I also didn't want to overwhelm her.

I was used to taking what I wanted. But not this time.

"First, the handfasting. It's a simple ritual that is only attended by close family. We promise to be with each other for one rotation and one day. A rotation is an Albyan year. We-"

"One *year*?" Jenny interrupted. "We're going to marry for one year only?"

I smiled at her confusion. "Let me finish. It's an old tradition that was primarily developed for couples who weren't biological mates. Not all Albyans find their true mates. Some don't even want to. They prefer to be with someone they like or love. The one year, one day period is to make sure both are ready to spend their entire life together. After that time has passed, they renew their vows."

Jenny cocked her head. "I suppose that would lower divorce rates a lot if people back home did that. I like it. And then there's a proper wedding after the first year?"

"The Bainnse ceremony, yes. Many more people attend, not just family but friends, acquaintances, local folks. Since this will be the first Bainnse in a generation, I assume it will be one big party." I took her wrists, enjoying the softness of her skin. "In the handfasting, our hands will be bound together with cloth. During the Bainnse, permanent marks will be placed where the cloth was a rotation and a day earlier. Every clan has their own design. When two clans unite through mating, their designs are combined into a new one. Since you're not Albyan, we will be able to be quite creative with that." I shrugged. "Not that I have a creative bone in my body."

Jenny chuckled. "My brother's wife is an artist. She paints in her free time and her paintings are good enough to sell. They used the proceeds from one of her artworks to pay for their honeymoon in the Galapagos – do you have honeymoons?"

"I'm not sure I understand. I tasted honey at breakfast on your planet, and Albya has three moons, but I don't see the connection."

She laughed again. I loved that sound. It made my antenna tingle pleasantly.

"A honeymoon is a holiday a newly married couple takes to spend some alone time with each other. Usually to a destination they wouldn't normally go."

"Ah, I see. We do not have a tradition like that, but I find the idea quite appealing. We can create a new custom for Peritan-Albyan couples."

Jenny looked down at her wrists which I still held in my hands. "How did we even get here? Are we really making wedding plans? I feel like we should slow down, but at the same time, I don't want to."

"I don't want to slow down, either," I admitted. "I need you, Jenny. I need to make you mine."

She smiled. "I think this is the moment where you kiss me."

"Is it?" I teased. "Maybe I should call my brother instead to schedule our handfasting ceremony."

Her eyes widened slightly, then sparkled with joy. "When?"

"Tomorrow? The only person I want to attend is Cyle. Maybe Vaxx. I wish your brother could join us, but it would take too long to fly him here. Besides, he doesn't yet know that I'm, well, not Peritan."

"We should rectify that soon. Can I call him later?"

"Of course. But first, I shall do as I'm told." I used my lower set of hands to gently push part her knees, allowing me to shuffle closer. She wrapped her legs around my waist. It felt natural. We were meant to be entwined like that.

With my upper set of arms, I cupped her face, pulling her so close that I could feel her breath on my cheeks. She smelled so good that I wanted to lick her skin, taste her like a morsel. Maybe I'd wait with that until later.

It was her who initiated the kiss. Her tongue swiped against my lips as if to say hello before her lips were on mine. She was all softness and warmth, so different from myself. I was a hard man, not just physically. I'd done things I wasn't proud of. I'd hurt people. Yet Jenny had slipped through the cracks of my rugged exterior, looked past my broken parts, and showed me that I was worth being with her. Yes, I truly believed that now. She'd healed me simply by being with me. My antenna would never grow back, but that didn't matter. I'd found my mate.

Her kiss was gentle yet passionate. I held back, resisting the urge to push her onto her back and ravage her mouth. I wanted her to feel like she was in charge. Because she was. I was hers to do with as she pleased.

Her hands ran over my back, releasing the tension I hadn't even noticed was there. Her tongue playfully danced with mine. And suddenly, her fingers wrapped around my broken antenna. I groaned. I couldn't hold back any longer.

I got to my feet, holding her in my arms, my lips never moving from hers. She was so light, so delicate. She'd lost some weight during our travel here and I'd make sure she regained it. I didn't want to break her.

My cock stood to attention. I was glad I didn't wear tight garments like the males on Peritus. My kilt didn't chafe or restrict my movement, but it didn't reduce the urge to plunge into Jenny, making her truly mine.

I broke the kiss, realising I was breathing hard. A fight wouldn't have got me out of breath like this, but Jenny had managed what none of my opponents ever did. She'd broken through my defences.

I hurried to the closest screen and used voice control to call my brother. Jenny laughed when she realised what I was doing.

"Is something wrong?" Cyle asked as soon as he appeared on the screen. His hair was tousled; he'd just come out of the bathing suite.

"I want to do the handfasting tomorrow. No. Tonight. Get an officiator and come here as soon as you can."

Cyle blinked at me as if I was speaking a different language. "Handfasting? Now? You?"

Jenny laughed. "I'm sure we can wait until tomorrow."

"No," I growled. My cock ached too much to wait that long. Every hour was going to be torture.

My brother still didn't look like he understood what was going on. For such an intelligent male, he could be slow on the uptake sometimes.

"Can you do it or not? I can get an officiator myself, but I thought you'd want to be there."

Cyle slowly shook his head. "Are you sure? Jenny, is this what you want?"

I growled again, anger rising up in me. "I would never force her."

Jenny stroked my cheek. "He wouldn't. It's what I want. But thanks for asking, Cyle. You're a good man."

"Tonight," I told Cyle before jealousy made me do something I'd regret. She'd called him a *good male*. I'd prove to her that I was the only male in her life. Sometimes good, sometimes wicked. And always hers.

14

Thorrn

Elder Havn himself had come with Cyle. Like me, both wore the traditional fly plaid over one shoulder, each with a brooch signifying their clan. Cyle's kilt was the same green pattern as mine, but once I was officially mated to Jenny, I might change that. I wanted a pattern just for us, just like the tattoos we'd get at the Bainnse. Maybe there were some symbols or colours from Peritus that Jenny wanted to add.

"Good evening to you," Havn greeted us as he stepped into my home. Usually, the ceremony would have been held in one of the ceremonial stone circles outside the city, but I was too impatient to fly there. We'd have our Bainnse there instead of in one rotation and one day.

"Does everyone on Albyan speak English?" Jenny whispered to me.

I laughed. "He was speaking Albyan Prime. And so are you."

She gaped at me. "What? I'm not. I'm talking English. I don't know any other languages. Well, some school French, but I've forgotten most of that."

"During our journey here, we attached a BrainTrain to you. It's a clever little device that uses subconscious programming. You now speak not only Albyan Prime but also the local dialect spoken in my village."

She looked both astonished and a little upset. "This BrainTrain, was it invasive? Is it some sort of implant?"

I shook my head and gently stroked her back to soothe her. "No, nothing like that. The transmission is done via earplugs that we removed as soon as we arrived here."

"Is that how you learned to speak English?"

"Yes. My brother already knew some of your language from his Peritan research, but the rest of us used BrainTrain devices."

"Wow," she muttered. "That's kind of unbelievable. I wish I'd had one of those things on Earth. I could have learned lots of languages, got a better job, walked in different circles, never met Jason..."

My mood darkened. "I wish you'd never met that male."

She smiled at me. "Let's forget about him. This is our evening."

"Yes. We will never speak his name again." I turned to Cyle and Havn. "Are you ready?"

Cyle pulled a small package from his bag. "I found our parents' handfasting cloth. I thought you might like to use it instead of something generic."

I gripped his forearms in thanks, moved by his thoughtfulness. "Thank you, brother."

I unwrapped the package, revealing the long strips of green cloth lined with golden thread. Their age was apparent, but when I touched them, I felt strangely connected with my parents. I wish they were here to witness their son claiming his mate. They would have loved Jenny. And they would be proud of me.

I turned away from the other males to hide my face. I didn't want them to see how emotional this made me. Jenny, however, was allowed to see this moment of weakness. She smiled up at me before inspecting the cloth.

"It's so beautiful. Was it made by hand?"

"Yes, my mother's mother's mother weaved it," I said, my voice strangely choked.

"It matches your eyes, just like your kilt."

Now she was making me embarrassed. I wasn't matching my eyes to my kilt, no, my kilt to my eyes. That wasn't something warriors did. Yet why did I feel flattered that she knew the colour of my eyes?

Jenny was wearing a simple white dress that the fabricator had finished creating just a few clicks before our guests had arrived. I'd warned her that I would be too impatient to undress her slowly. The dress would be torn apart. As a result, she'd chosen something simple from the fabricator's catalogue. For our Bainnse, she'd get the most elaborate dress with a sash in our colours, I'd make sure of that. I'd got a message an hour ago confirming that Jenny was getting a large compensation from the medpod's manufacturer. We were going to be able to afford whatever she wanted, plus the honeymoon she'd talked about. We could go to one of the resort planets if she wished.

"Where are we going to do the ceremony?" Havn asked, pulling me from my thoughts.

"In the courtyard outside. It's warm enough yet the breeze will keep any migges at bay." I didn't want to find out if these nasty little bloodsuckers liked to feast on Peritan females.

Cyle lent over to Jenny and whispered something in her ear. She nodded and smiled at him.

"What did he say?" I demanded, jealousy making my voice louder than I'd intended.

"I told her that I can give her a contraceptive injection," Cyle said, rolling his eyes at me. "I thought she might not want to breed right away."

Jenny blushed. I wanted to kiss her rosy cheeks. I loved when she changed colour like that.

"Ah. Good. Thank you."

Jenny held out her arm and Cyle pressed an injector to it. A blue light flashed and he pocketed the device with a satisfied grin. "You can come to me any time and I'll reverse the effect."

"Thanks, Cyle."

I took Jenny's hand and led her outside before my brother could distract her further. My house had been all she'd seen of Albya so far, but I'd rectify that soon enough. Tonight, she'd get to experience all parts and angles of my bed.

I adjusted the sporran dangling in front of my kilt, painfully bumping against my cock while I walked. I'd been hard all day. Being in Jenny's company did that.

The courtyard wasn't very big, but the two ancient trees in the centre made it feel cosy yet close to nature. Their entwined branches formed an archway under which Jenny and I came to stand. I handed Havn the cloth, pleased to see how reverently he handled it.

Cyle stood by the elder's side, grinning like a madman.

Havn cleared his throat. He was visibly moved. I had to remind myself that this was the first handfasting since the Sleep began. I knew he'd officiated mating ceremonies in the past, but it had been a long time since the last one.

"Have you, Jennifer MacPherson, freely agreed to become the mate of Thorrn of Clan Lannadh?"

"I have," she said in a strong, determined voice.

"Have you, Thorrn of Clan Lannadh, freely agreed to become the mate of Jennifer MacPherson?"

I took a deep breath. This was the most important moment of my life. "Aye, I have."

"Please hold out your hands," Havn asked.

Jenny extended her right arm and I held my left arms above and below hers. Havn raised the cloth to the evening sky.

"Upon this day, you will join as mates. For one rotation and one day, your lives will be entwined."

He slowly lowered the green band until it touched my upper wrist. I tangled my fingers with Jenny's, holding her tight. I was never going to let her go again.

"Upon this day, your souls will form an unbreakable knot."

Havn wrapped the cloth around our arms once, then twice. My heart thumped within my chest, bursting with emotion. With love for the female standing by my side.

"Upon this day, your bond will be as strong as this ribbon. You are now tied together, two beings as one, until you choose to renew your vows at the Stones of our ancestors or choose to walk separate ways."

He wrapped the ends of the cloth into a loose knot.

"Upon this day, you will claim each other as lawful mates." His eyes twinkled with mirth. "You may now leave us to complete the bond."

I was about to turn, desperate to get to the bedroom, when Jenny squeezed my hand.

"Wait. You have to kiss me first."

I looked down at her and smiled. "It will be my pleasure."

With my free arms, I snatched her up and pressed my lips to hers. This time, I took charge. With my kiss, I told her everything: how much I loved her, how much she meant to me, how I was the luckiest male in the universe.

I carried her into the house, never breaking the kiss, while cradling her in my arms like the precious treasure she was.

15

Jenny

He unwrapped the handfasting cloth and carefully folded it before setting it on a small shelf next to the bed. While I was still clinging to him like a monkey. Having four arms really came in handy.

My lips were swollen, my breath ragged and my skin flushed, and we hadn't done more than kissing. The first part of the ceremony was over and as beautiful and moving as it had been, I couldn't wait for the second part. I was quivering with need. My nipples were hard, pressing against the silky fabric of my dress.

"Are you happy?" he asked me suddenly. His eyes bored into me, seeking the truth.

I didn't have to think. "I couldn't be happier."

Thorrn raised an eyebrow. "No? Let's see if I can prove you wrong."

He flung me onto the bed, pushed up my dress and ripped off my panties, all so fast I couldn't process what had just happened. Cool air hit my exposed skin. I was wet and ready for him.

He pushed my thighs apart further before diving between my legs. When his tongue swiped across my folds, I moaned. Encouraged by that needy sound, he licked some more, swirling his tongue around my clit, sucking, lapping up my wetness. I clawed at the sheets, squirming beneath him. He strengthened his grip on my thighs, holding me in place. I didn't know how he knew exactly where to touch me, how he could play me like an instrument even though he'd never been with a woman, but I didn't care.

I cupped my breasts just so I had something to focus on, something that wasn't the blissful chaos erupting in my core.

"No," Thorrn whispered, his breath brushing against my bare pussy. "I'm the one who will please you tonight. Not you."

He sounded so serious, almost offended, that I had to laugh. I dutifully put my hands back on the sheets.

"Hands above your head. Let me look at you."

He got to his feet, towering above me. I wanted to move, get to my knees, touch him, but I kept still.

"Beautiful," he muttered and licked his lips. "But I need to see all of you."

In a flash, he was kneeling over me, his hands on my dress, and then it tore in the middle to the sound of seams ripping apart. His strength was incredible. He'd torn the dress in half without any visible effort. I was glad he'd warned me earlier. If this had been my own clothes from Earth, I may have been upset.

"So beautiful," he breathed and ran his hands over my body. I moaned and closed my eyes, giving in to the sensation of being touched all over. It was strange, having four hands caress me, as if I was with two men rather than one. I still hadn't seen what he was hiding beneath his kilt. Would there be two cocks? Or something else entirely? Soon.

I lost track of time and place. He explored my body, suckling on my hard nipples, pressing rows of kisses across my skin, and then one hand slid between my legs again. When he entered me with one finger, I bucked my hips, wanting more, so much more.

"Not yet," Thorrn whispered, his breath hot against my neck. "I'm not done preparing you yet."

"I need you," I moaned. "Fuck me."

"Patience." He kissed me on the mouth while his hands roamed my body. A second finger joined the first. I wasn't a virgin and I wasn't tighter than average, but his fingers were large and stretched me more than I'd thought. If he added a third, it would hurt. Not that I cared. I wanted him inside me.

"I love the way you arch your back when I do that," he said and sucked my nipple again, hard, his teeth grazing my sensitive flesh. I hadn't even realised I was doing it, but yet, he was right. I pushed my chest upwards to encourage him. He laughed and pinched my other nipple. I sucked in a sharp breath as pain and pleasure became one.

"You like that?"

I could only nod. Words were no more. He continued to play with my nipples, squeezing my breasts in between pinches and twists, while he fucked me with his fingers. I was close to coming. If he touched my clit one more time, there'd be no holding back. But I wanted to come with him inside me. Our first time. My first time with him.

"Stop," I managed to say.

He did so immediately. "Did I do something wrong?"

"No, the opposite. I'm so close. I want your cock. Please. Now. Before I come."

He didn't protest this time. He moved to the edge of the bed, my aching nipples forgotten. His hands spread my legs, then fingers pulled apart my pussy lips, opening me completely. The thick fabric of his kilt brushed my thighs, then he positioned himself against my entrance. He was big, hard and the thing I wanted most in the world.

"Mine," he groaned and pushed in. I screamed as he slipped inside, filling me to the brink. I felt so tight, so small compared to him. He gave me a moment to adjust, then pulled out ever so slowly. His hands were all over me again and with every touch, I got closer to the edge. I was burning with desire. He was everything I wanted and more.

"Don't hold back," I whispered hoarsely. "Fuck me."

The words were so crude, yet there was no other way to say it. I was driven by need and base instincts. All I wanted was for him to take me to that special place where I could float and cease to exist for a fraction of a second before coming back into reality renewed.

"My mate." He drove into me so hard his balls slapped against my thighs. He held me tight as he claimed me. I screamed, moaned, made noises I'd never made before.

And then his fingers found my clit and I broke apart. I rode the wave, barely conscious, the feeling of him pounding into me in the background. His hands found mine and I held onto him for dear life. My pussy clenched around him again and again while I kept shaking. No orgasm had ever been this intense. I arched my back and screamed when a second wave hit me, or maybe it was still the first, I didn't know. A strange vibration began within me, as if I had a vibe inside me instead of my mate's cock.

In one fluid motion, Thorrn raised my thighs, pulling up my arse, letting him push in even deeper. I hadn't thought that was possible. He groaned, guttural sounds coming from his throat. One last hard stroke and blazing heat filled me as he came with a scream. His fingernails buried into my thighs, but I didn't care. The vibrations around his cock's head slowed down just enough to stop me from going over the edge yet again.

He held me like that, embedded deep, his hot seed inside me. He seemed to have frozen.

I opened my eyes. A single tear ran down his cheek.

"What's wrong?" I whispered.

He simply looked at me. "Nothing. Nothing will be wrong ever again. I just... can't believe you're mine. My mate."

My heart threatened to explode with emotion. I hesitated to say what it was, but I knew it in my soul. Four tiny letters that meant so much.

Thorrn cleared his throat and wiped away the tear. "I love you, Jenny MacPherson."

Now I was almost crying myself. "I love you," I managed to say, my throat choking up. And it was true. I did love him. In the short time I'd known him, he'd taken root within my heart, my soul. I no longer doubted that we were meant for each other. We were mates and we'd always be mates.

I ended up curled against him, my eyes closed, simply enjoying his presence. He'd wiped me with a warm cloth before joining me on the bed. I was exhausted, my limbs heavy, but I'd never been happier.

I was already drifting asleep when something very important popped into my mind.

"I never saw!" I exclaimed.

"Saw what?"

I sat up and one of his hands immediately went to my lower back to steady me.

"Your kilt. I mean, what's under it." He was still wearing it. While I was completely naked, he'd only discarded his fly plaid. I supposed kilts were very handy for this sort of thing. I imagined how I could do the same, wear a skirt with nothing underneath, ready for him to bend me over a table and...

Thorrn laughed loudly. "Then you better take a look."

He didn't move, so I slowly pulled up his kilt myself, savouring the moment. By now, I knew that he only had the one cock, but that had been entirely enough for me. I wasn't greedy.

I gasped when I exposed his manhood. Ridges circled his shaft, turning an otherwise fairly human-shaped cock into something completely alien. His head was split into four parts with a small opening at the top where their tips came together. It reminded me of four flower petals that had folded together for the night. Would they... I wrapped my fist around him and the petals shook ever so slightly.

A groan escaped him. A challenge. I moved my hand up and down, slowly increasing the pressure. With every stroke, the petals opened a little further. And then they started vibrating. That explained the strange sensation while he'd fucked me. Wow. What would it feel like if I straddled him, holding him against my clit...

I was tired, but I couldn't resist. This was just too exciting.

I swirled my tongue over his head. He tasted like... maple syrup? Was that it? The petals moved under my touch, pressing against my tongue. I'd never felt anything like it. It was as if they wanted to be touched, wanted me to lick them. Of course that was rubbish. They were part of him. His cock. His beautiful, massive cock. And he was mine now.

I took him into my mouth, opening as wide as I could. How had he managed to fit into me? Even with the petals closed he was still far bigger than anything I'd ever had inside of me and that included the monster dildo I'd once bought online by mistake.

The petals pushed against the insides of my mouth as if they wanted to open.

"Jennnnny," Thorrn groaned. "What are you doing to me?"

I slowly pulled back. As soon as he popped out of my mouth, the petals shot open. I held a flower in my hand, one with a very, very thick stalk and the most beautiful four petals. They shimmered strangely silver as if someone had dunked the head of Thorrn's cock into metallic paint. I gently touched one with them. It trembled against my finger.

"Wow," I breathed. "You're so alien."

Thorrn chuckled, then groaned again when I ran my fingers over the petals in a circle. "It's not my fault your Peritan males aren't as well endowed. They don't seem to be built to please their females."

The petals' vibrations grew stronger as if they were begging for attention. I couldn't resist. I wanted to feel them inside of me again, especially now that I knew what his dick really looked like. The first time had been all about making Thorrn my mate. This time, it would be about exploring every single sensation this beautiful cock could give me.

I straddled him, slowly lowering myself until the petals touched my pussy. I was swollen and a little sore, but there was no way I was going to miss out on this.

"How do I make them close?" I asked. "They won't fit like this."

"You can't," Thorrn said, grinning widely. "But I can. The price is a kiss."

"That's extortion."

"No, it's not my fault you're so sgidding irresistible. I need to taste you again, mate."

He pushed himself up to make it easier for me to kiss him. The tip of one petal brushed against my clit and I moaned the very second Thorrn claimed my mouth. His hands went on my hips and pushed me back on his cock, not enough for it to enter me but enough for the petals to touch my pussy. No vibe would ever get close to what his cock was doing to me. It felt as if four tiny tongues were licking my clit, finding every sensitive spot, teasing me until I was close to erupting all over him.

"Stop," I moaned, breaking the kiss. "I need you now."

He reached between us and stroked his cock from the bottom up, closing his fist around the head. When he removed his hand, the petals were closed, although they were still shaking.

"I can't keep them like this for long." He fell back onto the mattress, breathing hard.

I gave him a wicked smile. "Then I better didn't keep you waiting."

I slowly lowered myself, giving myself time to adjust to his girth, taking him all in. It didn't feel like he'd already fucked me not long ago.

When I was fully seated on him, the vibrations started again. Something pushed against my cervix and my inner muscles clenched around his cock in response.

Thorrn groaned, throwing his head back. I smiled and started to fuck him, swaying my hips, moving up and down a little, riding his cock. My breasts whipped up and down as I increased my pace.

I felt powerful. Here I was, on top of my alien mate, in complete control.

The ridges along his cock rubbed against my clit, bringing me ever closer to the point of no return.

"I'm close," I warned him. I put my hands on his chest to steady myself. He took that as a sign to take over. He gripped my hips tightly and pushed me down onto his cock. His balls slapped against my pussy at the same time as the vibrations inside me reached a new level of intensity. It was enough to drive me over the edge.

I came with a scream, my nails biting into his skin as I searched for something to hold on to. I clenched around him, my inner muscles milking his cock, and then he came too, roaring like an animal, shooting his hot seed into my waiting pussy. The petals pushed outwards, connecting us, locking him in place. Their vibrations made me shiver with the aftershocks of my orgasm, almost making me come a second time.

Thorrn sat up, wrapped his arms around me, pushing himself even deeper. We clung to each other, our hips moving in a slow dance. I closed my eyes and buried my face in his braided hair, breathing in his scent. Inside me, his cock pulsed, reminding me that we belonged together.

"How long will it stay like this?" I whispered after a while. It could have been seconds, minutes or hours. I had no sense of time left. All that mattered was his presence, his touch.

"Usually, about one intergalactic hour. Because it's our first time, probably a lot longer." He chuckled. "My cock is getting to know your tight little pussy. It feels so good. I never want this to end."

"Me neither. And it doesn't have to."

"You're right."

He gently lowered us back onto the bed and onto the side. My legs were still wrapped around him while his arms held me in a warm, comforting embrace. I pressed small kisses to his naked skin while my mind drifted.

"Satisfied?" he muttered with a chuckle.

"For now. If I wasn't so tired, I'd find out what more you can do."

He grinned at me, flashing his teeth, all predator. "I will show you as soon as you wake up. You're my mate now. You shall know my body as well as I know yours." His fingers tangled my hair. "But now, you need to rest. Sleep, little female. I'm going to watch over you while you recover your strength."

I closed my eyes and gave into exhaustion. His cock was deep inside me, binding us together like the handfasting cloth. We belonged together. He was mine and I was his.

His scent surrounded me like a warm blanket. I was safe with him. I loved him. And in a year and one day, I would renew my vows and we'd be mates for the rest of our lives.

EPILOGUE
FOUR WEEKS LATER

Jenny

P am fussed with her hair.

"You look fine," I told her. "None of these males will care about your hair. They know that you're married and off-limits."

She smirked, still running her hands through her hair. "Some days, I wish I wasn't. Having those Highlander posters above my desk can be quite distracting. My husband has already told me that he's getting himself a kilt."

I laughed. "Yes, I can confirm that Albyans can be very distracting." Thorrn chuckled from my right, but I pointedly ignored him. I was still sore from this morning's bedroom adventures.

"Sign-ups are through the roof. Half of Scotland seems to have signed up to be matched. I've had to hire two new assistants to help with all the applications. Even so, it's going to take us weeks to deal with the backlog. We've turned off the website form until we're all caught up."

"The Albyans will be pleased to hear it. They're desperate for the first females to get here. Are you ready for the clan elders to be added to the call? And stop fussing with your hair!"

Pam straightened and finally put her hands in her lap. "Ready. I think. This is a little overwhelming."

Cyle had told her the truth before we'd left Earth, but he'd never shown her his true form. Last week, I'd persuaded Thorrn to join us in our chat and yes, I'd been rather proud of him presenting his spectacular physique. By now, I was used to his four arms and couldn't imagine ever going back to a mate with only two.

Thorrn did something on his commstick and the screen in front of me splintered into thirteen images with Pam in the centre. Her eyes widened slightly when she saw all those males looking at her with curiosity. She was only the second human they'd ever seen, so it was understandable that they were intrigued. Pam was older than me and her hair was streaked with grey. Small wrinkles surrounded her eyes and mouth, both from age and laughing.

Elder Havn cleared his throat. "Thank you for this meeting. I was hoping you'd be able to give us an update on how things are progressing on your end."

Pam inclined her head. "Certainly. We've now got about four hundred women in our database. A third of them have given us DNA samples. I'm just waiting for the lab to analyse them so I can send you the data. But I've already sent Cyle ten DNA reports that I had fast-tracked."

Cyle, on a screen just above Pam, smiled in approval. "I'm almost certain I have identified the sequence in Jenny's genome that marks her compatibility with Thorrn. I looked for the same marker in the ten data sets and think I have found matches among Albyan males."

Gasps followed his words. If Cyle hadn't told me the good news over breakfast, I would have been just as shocked as everyone else.

"I vote we invite a group of Peritan females to Albya," Cyle continued. "It will help me confirm if my matching algorithm is correct."

"We will send a ship right away," Havn said. His antennae were wobbling with excitement. I'd learned that older Albyans sometimes lost control of their antennae when they got emotional. "Cyle, keep the names of the males to yourself for now. We don't want to cause too much excitement and jealousy until the females arrive and we can be certain that they really are matches."

Cyle inclined his head. "I agree."

One by one, the clan elders logged off until only Pam and Cyle remained.

"Brother," Cyle said with a wry smile. "I think you will be best placed to talk to one of the males."

Thorrn stopped preparing our lunch and leaned over my shoulder. "Why?"

"Because one of them is Eron."

My mate groaned.

"What is it?" I asked.

"Eron is... different.

Cyle laughed. "That's one way of describing him. He's a hermit who runs a taigeis farm in the middle of nowhere. I very much hope that whatever female he's matched with loves the countryside."

"A taigeis farm?" I repeated. "I want to go!"

While I'd refused to eat their meat, I'd wanted to cuddle one of the fluffy animals ever since Thorrn had shown me a holo version on his commstick.

Thorrn pulled me from my chair and slid his lower arms around my waist. "Didn't you mention that

Peritans go on holiday after their mating ceremony? I think I know where we will go."

He spun me around and kissed me. I ignored Pam's chuckles and gave myself to my mate. One of his hands slipped under my skirt and I knew lunch would have to wait. I returned the favour, lifting his kilt just enough to grasp his thick manhood.

"Don't do that, mate," he whispered hoarsely.

I blinked up at him, all innocence. "Why not?"

"Because it reminds me of how much I love you. And how much I want to mark you as mine after having all those males look at you."

"You're such a caveman."

Thorrn pressed a quick kiss on my lips. "Then let me take you to my cave."

He lifted me into his arms and carried me into the bedroom.

Our honeymoon would have to wait.

Get an exclusive bonus scene set during their second honeymoon a year later:
skyemackinnon.com/thorrn-bonus

You may have already realised that the next book in the

Starlight Highlanders series is all about Eron, the taigeis farmer, and the woman sent to stay with him – who's not happy about being matched with an alien instead of the hot HUMAN Highlander she expected.

Get your copy of Eron: books2read.com/eron

Want to know more about Thorrn's brother Cyle and how he finds his mate?
He's also got his own book: books2read.com/cyle

Would you like your own Albyan Highlander? Join the Hot Tatties Dating Agency:
skyemackinnon.com/hottatties

Want to know what he's hiding under that kilt?
Go to my website to find out!
(*definitely not safe for work*)

skyemackinnon.com/starlightnsfw

AUTHOR'S NOTE

Dear readers,

This book has been such great fun to write. I loved every minute of it and can't wait to explore more of Albya in the next book (Eron). The taigeis on Eron's farm are super cute and I'd give anything to have one myself. My friend Arizona drew me one, isn't it adorable?

I'd been wanting to write about 'Scottish' aliens for ages, so when I got the chance to write a series for the Intergalactic Dating Agency, there was no stopping me. I live on the West coast of Scotland with a view of both rolling green hills and a sea loch – the perfect inspiration. I rarely have men in kilts walking past my window, but during the summer I do occasionally get to see topless males on the seafront. Passers-by, please be assured that none of you were the model for Thorrn.

I have a few apologies to get off my chest:

First, to my Gaelic teacher. I took some Gaelic lessons a few years ago and have a book full of Gaelic swearwords that came in very handy when developing the Albyan language (The Naughty Little Book of Gaelic, highly recommended!). I'm not sure my Gaelic teacher would appreciate what I did with this beautiful language, but I couldn't resist. Tha mi duilich.

I'd also like to apologise to my friends and my wonderful assistant Tricia for sending them random ideas and snippets every day or two. I get passionate about my characters and sometimes overshare.

Now on to the positive acknowledgements. I'd like to thank the fabulous other IDA authors who invited me into their midst. I'm honoured to be part of the project.

Thank you to my mother and sister for not reading this book.

(if you're reading this, please don't tell me)

The biggest thanks goes to my cat Sootie who always makes sure to delete unnecessary paragraphs by walking over the keyboard. She's the best editor you can imagine.

Take care,

Skye

PS You can get both signed paperbacks and swag for this series in my shop: **Perytonpress.com/store**

INTERGALACTIC DATING AGENCY

Looking for a love that's out of this world? These strong, smart, sexy aliens are seeking mates from the Milky Way. Just hop onboard with your local Intergalactic Dating Agency! Join a crew of rock star Sci Fi Romance authors as we explore the friendly skies and beyond with trilogies of cosmic craving, astral adventure and otherworldly lovers. Warning: abductions may or may not be included!

Grab more hunky alien action here: romancingthealien.com

ABOUT THE AUTHOR

Skye MacKinnon is a USA Today & International Bestselling Author whose books are filled with strong heroines who don't have to choose.

She embraces her Scottishness with fantastical Scottish settings and a dash of mythology, no matter if she's writing about Celtic gods, cat shifters, or the streets of Edinburgh.

When she's not typing away at her favourite cafe, Skye loves dried mango, as much exotic tea as she can squeeze into her cupboards, and being covered in pet hair by her tiny demonic cat.

Subscribe to her newsletter:
skyemackinnon.com/newsletter

facebook.com/skyemackinnonauthor

twitter.com/skye_mackinnon

instagram.com/skyemackinnonauthor

bookbub.com/authors/skye-mackinnon

goodreads.com/SkyeMacKinnon

tiktok.com/@skyemackinnonauthor

ALSO BY

Find all of Skye's books on her website, skyemackinnon.com, where you can also order signed paperbacks and swag. Many of her books are available as audiobooks.

Science Fiction Romance

Set in the Starlight Universe

- **Starlight Monsters** (sci-fi m/f romance)
- **Starlight Highlanders Mail Order Brides** (sci-fi m/f romance, part of the Intergalactic Dating Agency)
- **The Intergalactic Guide to Humans** (sci-fi romance with various pairings)

Set in other worlds

- **Between Rebels** (sci-fi reverse harem set in the Planet Athion shared world)
- **The Mars Diaries** (sci-fi reverse harem)
- **Aliens and Animals** (f/f sci-fi romance co-written with Arizona Tape)
- **Through the Gates** (dystopian reverse harem co-written with Rebecca Royce)

Paranormal & Fantasy Romance

- **Claiming Her Bears** (post-apocalyptic shifter reverse harem)
- **Daughter of Winter** (fantasy reverse harem)
- **Catnip Assassins** (urban fantasy reverse harem)
- **Infernal Descent** (paranormal reverse harem based on Dante's Inferno, co-written with Bea Paige)
- **Seven Wardens** (fantasy reverse harem co-written with Laura Greenwood)
- **The Lost Siren** (post-apocalyptic, paranormal reverse harem co-written with Liza Street)

Other Series

- **Academy of Time** (time travel academy standalones, reverse harem and m/f)
- **Defiance** (contemporary reverse harem with a hint of thriller/suspense)

Standalones

- Song of Souls – m/f fantasy romance, fairy tale retelling

- Their Hybrid – steampunk reverse harem
- Partridge in the P.E.A.R. - sci-fi reverse harem co-written with Arizona Tape
- Highland Butterflies – lesbian romance
- Storm Witch - historical paranormal reverse harem

Anthologies and Box Sets

- Hungry for More – charity cookbook
- Daggers & Destiny – a Skye MacKinnon starter library

Printed in Great Britain
by Amazon

87249455R00109